11/24

The Cabinet of Wonders

2. Lisi

The Cabinet of Wonders
2. Lisi

Ellis Delmonte

The Cabinet of Wonders : 2. Lisi
Ellis Delmonte

She opened her eyes, or thought she did, because what she saw couldn't be real. The arch was no longer white. All the colours of the rainbow raced through it, alive with light, and through this shimmering, glimmering rainbow, Lisi saw something that took her breath away.

Lisi is next to own a Cabinet of Wonders and this time there's a crystal prism at its heart...

For
Shira and Neomi

The Cabinet of Wonders : 2. Lisi

Text copyright©2016 Ellis Delmonte
Cover design©2016 Ian Purdy
ISBN 978-1-908577-53-5

First published as The Fantastic Prismatic Construction Kit
ISBN ISBN 978-0-9566342-0-7 in 2010

This Edition 2016

5 3 1 2 4

British Library Cataloguing in Publication Data.
A catalogue record for this book is available from the
British Library.

Hawkwood Books 2016

1. Blue Sky Thinking

Lisi lay back on the grass, staring at a wispy white cloud drifting lazily across an otherwise clear cobalt sky. The vast emptiness was hypnotic, giddily high, yet she felt she could touch it. She reached towards the silvery shreds of the cotton wool wonder but it evaded her outstretched hand and continued on its way.

"Do you mind being all by yourself?" she asked the shape-shifting cloud. It didn't answer. "I don't," she said. "I don't mind at all."

Whether that was true or not, only she knew, and even she didn't know for sure. She was all of twelve years old, an orphan of war and ever so slightly peculiar, as she heard people say. People, not friends. Friends were few and far between, so far that sometimes she couldn't see one even if she squinted beyond the horizon.

This was the place where being alone felt okay, in the garden of her foster home. It was a long, partly wild garden with some decent private spots away from the house. Effem or Effdee sometimes wandered down to see what she was doing, but generally they let her be. They were letting her be now and she was enjoying the sky, the cloud and the light.

She loved the light, almost as much as she feared the dark. She wondered where it came from, all that brightness, and how it could change itself into greens and blues and yellows and a million other astonishing colours.

She also wondered, though she tried not to, how it could all be turned in a mad, bad second, to ash. She knew it could happen because she'd seen it. Colour after colour burned to cinder until light itself was extinguished. Even now, so long after seeing what she'd seen, she feared that this bright, magical world would burn to blisters, that some stupid grown-up would find a reason to raze it to the ground in blinding flames.

She could handle the memories here, where there was space and light and colour, but she couldn't handle it at night, alone in her bedroom, even when Effem or Effdee sat with her. That was too much. The blasts and the fire ripped through her mind and scared her more than any silly stories. War scared her more than all the monsters in the universe because it was real.

"No bad thoughts," the cloud said, "not on such a day as this!"

She had to agree, it was a spectacular day. Apart from that single, talkative cloud, the sky was a magnificent shade of blue.

It reminded her of something Effdee had said in a meeting a few months ago when he'd taken her to work. There were all these important people sitting around a giant table listening to her father who had told them to use 'blue sky thinking'. Lisi had wondered what it meant, and she hadn't understood when Effdee tried to explain on the way home, but now she did - it meant thinking clearly. She agreed, it was very important to think as clearly as a bright blue sky, even if there was a wispy cloud in the way.

"I'll be gone soon," it said.

She didn't mind it being there; it gave her something to focus on, otherwise she might have felt even more dizzy staring at the tremendous nothingness of space.

Hmm. Clear thinking might be important but it wasn't easy. People were too complicated for that. Nobody had taught her this, but she knew it. If people were straightforward she'd be living with her real parents in her own country and everything would be hunky-dory, but they weren't, and she wasn't, and that was that.

"I'm going," said the cloud.

"I can see," said Lisi.

The wispy thread of white was drifting away, leaving behind a dazzlingly pure bowl of inky blue heaven.

Lisi felt tiny, a frail slip of a girl, light as the proverbial feather, stuck to the Earth as it floated through space. Why didn't she fall off, she wondered? After all, the Earth was round and she was just as much underneath it as on top of it. She wouldn't have minded falling off. She could drift away like that cloud, somewhere nice and peaceful where people didn't fight with each other all the time.

But she didn't fall off. Something held her to the ground, and if she concentrated hard she could almost feel it, a pressure of some kind, like an invisible hand pinning her down.

"Lisi?"

She heard Effem's voice as if it had come from another planet, she was so lost in her thoughts.

"There you are!"

Effem was all love and compassion, sometimes too

much of it, forgetting the heart space Lisi still needed. Lisi sat up and looked at Laura, her Foster Mum, otherwise known as Effem.

"What are you doing?"

"Looking at the sky and thinking."

"Nice thoughts?"

"Some of them."

Laura and Adam had always wanted a child but they couldn't have one of their own, so when they heard of Lisi's plight they made a decision and here she was, their adopted daughter. She sat down on the grass facing Lisi.

"Penny for them?"

Lisi shook her head.

"I'm alright, honestly."

Laura wasn't sure if Lisi was alright or not. She was such a quiet girl, always thinking, probably about her real mum and dad, certainly about the the rough things she'd seen. Laura and Adam were good people, but they were torn apart when it came to their distant, adopted girl. They wanted the best for her, but if the best meant that her real parents ever reappeared, then they weren't sure if they could bear losing her, but all they wanted was what was best for her, not what was best for them. It had been nine months, so the chances were small, but not impossible. It could still happen. Lisi's war torn home was healing. Her parents might be alive and searching for her that very moment.

"Adam and I were thinking," said Laura, "if you'd like to go to the seaside for a few days."

"Why?" Lisi asked.

"Why? Well, because it would make a change. You

could see the sea and go to the fun fair. You might make some new friends, you never know. It would be a break."

Lisi thought for a moment and then said, "Alright. Thank you."

Laura was surprised. She'd expected her to say no, but Lisi was nothing if not unpredictable. Her head was about as busy as any head could be, but this was a quick and good decision.

"You're always so polite Lisi," laughed Laura. "We'll go tomorrow. It will be exciting! Thank *you*!" she said.

Lisi had only ever seen the sea from the boat that brought her to England from the fighting she was trying so hard to forget. It was like the sky, in a way, too big and mysterious to understand. She stood up, walked back to the house and into the kitchen where Laura was making supper.

"What's it like," Lisi asked, "the seaside?"

Laura stopped stirring and said, "A fun place. Lots to do. Lots to see."

Lisi had a picture in her head of what it might be like. It sounded... interesting. She felt a momentary thrill of anticipation, something she hadn't known for a long while.

"You might even win something," said Laura.

Lisi took that thought to her room. She'd never won anything in her life, and during the terrible fighting she'd felt as if she was losing everything. She knelt on her bed looking out of the window into the garden, trying not to remember the dark things, just the good, but it was difficult. She rubbed the window with her sleeve to remove some dust but there was dust inside her head just as much as on the glass. She saw things she didn't want to see and heard things she didn't want to hear, as if the world in front of her eyes was only a small part of the real story. Her memory and her funny-peculiar brain were much more real. How could you not have bad memories and a stubborn, solitary mind when you'd seen what she'd seen? It wasn't possible.

She knew what would make her happy - having a proper friend, someone who said the right things, did the right things and didn't make her feel so... so alone. Everyone did that, though they didn't mean to. They were all so happy, and she wasn't, and they didn't understand. She wondered if she was normal, if she would ever be normal, so that other children would want to be her friend rather than shy away, which was what they seemed to do.

She longed to see things properly again. Maybe the seaside would help. The problem with having seen what she'd seen was that the memories followed you around. You saw everything as if you were looking through a grubby window or darkened glass. You couldn't get away from it. You could run away shouting and screaming or sulk and mope but none of it made an ounce of difference because you were who you were and what had been done could never be undone.

If her real mum and dad came back from the ruins of their home, if that miracle happened, then she might start over and be different, but that was about as likely as her winning something special at the seaside funfair.

2. Jackpot

It was a crazy place. For some reason, Lisi had imagined a balmy beach with vast stretches of sand and a small fun fair, but actually it was vast stretches of fun fair and a small stony beach.

She'd never seen anything like it. There were lights everywhere, not hundreds, not thousands, but countless numbers of them, all shapes, sizes and colours, some still, some flashing, everyone of them screaming at her, 'Look at me!'

She couldn't take it all in.

The sounds were equally disturbing, a cacophony of whizzing, buzzing, ringing, shouting and yelling.

'I don't like it Laura,' she wanted to say, but she knew that Laura and Adam were doing their best to cheer her up and she didn't want to seem ungrateful. She stood between them for comfort as they wandered around, hardly knowing what to do first. There were so many games and rides, you couldn't look at one without being distracted by another. It took a long time to get used to the pandemonium.

They went on the Big Wheel first because it was fairly slow and gave them a wide panorama of the fair and the sea. Lisi looked down, not afraid at all of the height, fascinated by the carpet of colour below. She squeezed Laura's hand, suddenly remembering other panorama's of light which hadn't been so friendly.

"Are you alright, sweety?" Laura asked.

Lisi nodded, but she was trying to push out of her mind the blasts of exploding light and sound that had stolen her childhood away. This was different, she told herself. She was safe here.

As they rose into the air, the noise dwindled and the flashing forest of neon lights grew less threatening.

They went around three times and each time she felt more comfortable higher up than close to the ground. She was much less afraid than Laura who closed her eyes at the top, gripping the safety bar so tightly that the veins in her hand began to bulge.

The next ride was much more daunting, so much so that Laura decided to let Adam and Lisi go alone. It was a vertical drop from a dizzy height, like a lift where the cable had broken. It rose slowly and hung at the top, way above the ground. There was no warning, just a sudden siren and then a rapid plummet downwards. Lisi didn't make a sound. Virtually everyone else on the ride yelled and screamed with fear and excitement but Lisi was thinking that despite the sudden fall, this was still safe.

She knew what it was like not to be safe, when explosions and screams were real, when life itself was threatened, so this was make-believe, even if her tummy did try to push its way through her head.

The ghost train was relatively peaceful after the two giant rides. Things bumped into her and tickled her and tried to scare her, but she wasn't scared at all. Laura was anxious, but about Lisi, not the scary ride. She wondered what would bring the girl back into the world, the adorable child, so bright, so beautiful and so firmly clamped shut.

They had some candy floss and sat down to rest, watching the crowds go by, family after family, an endless sea of people, all alive with the fun of the fair. But little Lisi watched them like she would watch television or read a book, knowing she wasn't part of it. A couple of girls smiled at her but she looked away, unwilling to talk.

"Enjoying it?" Adam asked. Lisi nodded, but it was always embarrassing when Effdee or Effem asked her if she was enjoying something. She would invariably say yes because if she said no, then it sounded rude. She wasn't *not* enjoying it, she just wasn't part of it.

They stopped at a few games, like catching numbered fish from a tiny pond or throwing hoops over blocks. Lisi won nothing. She tried her luck at a mechanical crane, aiming to hook some novelty prizes. After three goes she gave up, thinking it was impossible, but she watched a boy have a go next and he picked up a prize first time.

"It's just luck," said Laura, beginning to think that Lisi's sadness was affecting her chances at winning anything at all. Then they tried Roll-a-Penny, only it wasn't a penny, it was ten pence. You could spend a fortune there if you had the money, and probably even if you didn't have the money. The idea was to roll a penny into a moving pile of coins that eventually tipped over the edge into a collecting tray. The pile seemed large and unstable, as if it could collapse any moment, but every coin they rolled down just added to the pile and never seemed to push it further. They heard sounds of people collecting winnings, and a couple of times they got a few coins back, but not many, and some of them were old coins no longer in circulation. Nevertheless, it was entertaining.

They found their way to a small, noisy arcade full of one armed bandits, crunching, clanging machines that stole from the poor to give to the rich. The manager smiled at them as they came in. They knew he was the manager because he wore a silver badge with "Manager" written on it, a complete giveaway.

Lisi had never seen arcade machines before and was fascinated. Laura and Adam decided to sit this one out and let Lisi wander round alone, safe enough as there was only one way in or out. They gave her five pounds and said that when the money was used up, which it undoubtedly would be, she should come back to the entrance to meet them.

Lisi wandered around, watching how intently the customers played the machines. She was confused by the lights and the noise and didn't think she would be able to understand what to do, but she saw an empty booth at the far end and settled herself down on the rotating stool.

It was a good choice. She felt very comfortable and studied the instructions on the glass top of the bandit. It was fairly straightforward - put your money in, ten pence at a time, pull the handle and hope for the best. If you got three in a row of anything you would win a prize. These prizes varied depending on the pictures, so oranges and apples were common and three of those wouldn't get you much. Strawberries were better and grapes better still, but neither offered treasure chests of gold. There was a bell, and three of those looked promising, but the rarest picture of all was a bar with

'Jackpot' written on it. Three of those wouldn't do you any harm. You could nudge the dials if the 'nudge' light came on so there was a little skill involved, but mainly it was Lady Luck.

When she was ready, Lisi dropped in her first ten pence piece and pulled the handle, watching the dials with their colourful pictures race around. When they stopped, she saw one bar with 'Jackpot' – good start, but then grapes and an orange. Hmm. She nudged the grape to make another orange but two oranges weren't worth anything and there was no other Jackpot in sight.

She slotted in another ten pence piece, and then another and another. There was something very comforting about pulling the handle and watching the dials spin around. Each time she did it, she listened to the whirring machine, wondering what was going on inside, losing herself in the mysterious appeal of fickle fortune.

The fifth time she put in a coin, she got three oranges and won three ten pence pieces. That was something. She felt like a winner even if she was losing, and it went on that way for quite a while. She would lose sixty or seventy pence, then win twenty or thirty. Occasionally she would see the Jackpot bar appear, but never more than one at a time. She wondered whether there were truly three of them on the dials – she never saw it on the middle one, only on the left and right. She was four pounds down when Laura and Adam came to see how she was doing.

"That's why it's called a one arm bandit," said Adam. "Had enough?"

Lisi shook her head.

"Just one pound left," said Laura, "you don't want to waste it on this, do you Sweetie?"

Actually, she did.

"No more money," said Adam, showing his empty pockets.

Lisi asked if she could stay another five minutes and so they left her, wondering if their adopted daughter was becoming a gambler. Lisi screwed up her nose at the machine and dropped in another ten pence piece.

Orange, apple and grape.

Rubbish.

Another coin.

Apple, grape, grape.

Nudge.

Strawberry, grape, grape.

Still rubbish.

She put the next few coins in and watched intently as the same old fruits popped up. Before she knew it, she had only one coin left. She stared at the machine as if questioning why it was so mean, but she wasn't angry or unhappy. She might have been, but she wasn't. She seemed to accept that this was the way it worked and that you had to be extraordinarily lucky to win anything at all, and probably, even if you won, you'd soon put the money back trying to win more.

She dropped in the last coin, blew the machine a gentle kiss, and pulled the handle.

One Jackpot appeared.

Good.

Another Jackpot appeared, and in the middle.

Excellent.

Then an orange.

Oh well.

But she saw the nudge light flashing in the third column and beneath the orange was a third Jackpot bar. She pressed the nudge button, unable to remember which way the nudge button pushed the display, sure it was the wrong way, but it wasn't, and Lisi found herself staring at three Jackpot bars in a beautifully straight line, staring back at her as if to say, 'Thank you for blowing us a kiss. This is for you.'

Suddenly the silence of the booth exploded with noise. Bells rang, hooters hooted and dozens of people gathered around to see what had happened. Lisi sat on the stool, unsure what to do. She expected piles of money to come tumbling into the tray, but nothing appeared, not even a one pence piece.

As suddenly as the noise had begun, it stopped, and just as it stopped, Lisi saw something drop into the collection tray.

It wasn't money. It was a reddish, round, plastic token with an antique cabinet engraved on one side and a face on the other. It was quite cheery but it didn't look as though it was worth much. People gathered around stared at it, and at Lisi, and started muttering things like, "Ooh, that's a bit of a cheat," and "Ooh, what's that?" and "Ooh, how peculiar!"

Lisi liked the feel of it in the palm of her hand. It was warm, perhaps because it had been sitting in the machine for a long time, and comforting. Something different. She heard her name called and turned to see Effem and Effdee pushing their way through the crowds of curious onlookers.

"Lisi, are you okay?"

"I won," she said, simply.

The Jackpot signs were still flashing but the collection tray was empty.

"What did you win?" Laura asked, puzzled.

"This," said Lisi, showing her the token.

Laura and Adam studied it.

"That face..." said Adam. "I seem to recognise it."

Then it dawned on him.

"It's the manager!" he said. "I'm sure it is!"

They left the booth, someone else immediately grabbing Lisi's place and setting the machine in motion, but the Jackpot signs spun away and probably never lined themselves up in the same way ever again.

The cashier looked at the token, then at Lisi and the two adults, picked up the phone and pressed a button. They heard her mutter something into the mouthpiece. A door opened and a rough looking man came out.

"What?" he said brusquely.

They were taken aback by his tone but showed him the token. He seemed to relent slightly and ushered them into a small, comfortable room where the manager greeted them.

"Forgive Peter's brusqueness," he said. "Peter," he said, "do learn to tell the difference between good and bad. It's quite easy, you know."

Peter looked sheepish but was obviously more used to dealing with scoundrels and troublemakers than children like Lisi. He went a deep shade of red and left the room.

"My name is Angel," said the manager, "in charge," he said, pointing to his badge. "And you are?"

"Lisi," said Lisi.

"And your parents?"

"Foster parents," said Adam.

"I see," said Mr Angel. "Now, the token, please."

Lisi handed it to him and Mr Angel inspected it, sitting on the edge of his grand desk.

"Excellent," he said, "very well done. Looks a little like me as I was many years ago," he added ruefully, studying the face on the token. "Age does no one any favours, don't you agree?"

"Effdee recognised you," said Lisi. "You can't have changed that much," at which the manager laughed and said he wasn't sure whether that was a compliment or not. "Have I won something?" Lisi asked, naturally curious about all this.

"Indeed you have," said the manager. "These tokens are quite rare, you know."

"Jackpots can't be that rare," said Adam.

"Jackpots, quite rare, believe me, but tokens, oh yes, very rare and very selective. Let me see."

He dropped it into a machine on his desk, something like a fax machine, only it wasn't a fax. You generally don't drop tokens into fax machines and fax machines never burp out golden announcement cards like this:

You have won our special
JACKPOT PRIZE
which will be delivered to your home at
12 o'clock precisely tomorrow.
Be there or be square.

The manager gave the card to Lisi who looked at it, as puzzled as she was before.

"What is it?" she asked.

"It's a card," said the manager.

"No, the prize," said Lisi.

"Ah, well that would be telling," he said. "It's our top jackpot prize. You won't be disappointed."

"This is a bit... unusual," said Laura.

"Oh no," said the manager, "not 'a bit unusual', it's *highly* unusual. It's about as unusual as you can imagine."

"Couldn't we just take it with us," said Adam.

"Afraid not," said the manager, "it isn't here, you see. This is a special jackpot, we don't keep it on the premises."

He looked at Lisi kindly and said, "I'm glad it's you. You look like a very pleasant young lady. So, are you excited?"

Lisi nodded, although she was more puzzled than excited. She wasn't an expert on arcade games but she suspected that this wasn't the normal way to win a jackpot.

The manager chatted to them for a while, asking friendly questions and answering many more. He seemed delighted with Lisi, congratulated her again and told the family to make sure they were ready for delivery of the jackpot prize at the given time.

They were, all three of them on tenterhooks wondering what was going to be delivered.

"I've never heard of anything like it," said Laura.

"We should tell the papers," said Adam.

"We should wait and see," said Lisi, sensibly.

They waited patiently, regularly checking the time until they heard the midday chimes on the radio. And then the most unexpected thing happened.

Nothing at all.

Mr Angel had been so open and honest, none of them had doubted that Lisi's prize would be delivered at twelve, but twelve passed, a minute, then two, then five, then fifteen, and there was no knock at the door, no ringing of the bell, nothing.

They looked at each other, speechless.

"They may be held up in traffic," said Laura.

"They would have called," said Adam.

"It doesn't matter," said Lisi. "I don't mind. It was fun just winning, even if I didn't actually win anything."

Adam put his hand on her shoulder and squeezed it.

"No sweetheart," he said, "we can't have you growing up thinking that adults are fibbers and the world is a cheat. This isn't right. You won a prize and you'll get it."

"But how?" said Lisi?

Adam thought about this, and so did Laura who was livid. She had no words to describe her anger at this terrible let-down. How could Mr Angel – ha! what a misleading name! – lie to someone like Lisi? What a monster he must be, out to make money and cheat little children!

"We'll report him to the police!" she said.

"Yes," said Adam, "but first we'll pay him a visit. I'll drive down there tomorrow morning, first thing. I'll take time off work and give him a piece of my mind."

"Can't we phone him?" Lisi asked.

Adam looked at Laura. Neither of them had the number, and besides, they doubted such a monster would be easy to reach on the phone.

What a sham!

What a fake!

They didn't leave the house during the afternoon, just in case the delivery turned up late, but it didn't. The hours passed and nothing arrived, no courier, no post, not the least sniff of a sausage.

Laura and Adam were both upset and angry. They loved Lisi as if she was their real daughter and they knew what she'd been through, so they were doubly incensed. As for Lisi herself, she wasn't angry at all. She knew more about the disappointments of life than most people, even though she was so young, and she'd half expected this, so she went out into the garden, read a book, talked to a couple of clouds, came inside and did some schoolwork, watched television and then went to bed hoping that Effdee wouldn't get into trouble when he confronted the manager.

Despite the disappointment, they all dropped off to sleep quickly and were deep in the Land of Nod at midnight when the doorbell rang.

3. The Cabinet of Wonders

Effdee opened the door in his dressing gown with Laura standing next to him and Lisi behind both of them, wide awake. They had looked through the spyhole and seen Mr Angel standing there with two men, all in smart courier uniforms, and in between them, on the ground, a huge crate.

They opened the door on a chain so and peeked through the gap.

"Twelve o'clock," said Mr Angel. "I thought you'd all be up and about!"

"It's twelve midnight," said Adam. "We thought you meant twelve noon."

"Twelve noon!" exclaimed Mr Angel. "What sort of time is that to deliver a jackpot prize like this? No, twelve midnight!"

He had a twinkle in his eye which suggested that he knew very well what was going on and what they'd thought of him. They opened the door and the three men heaved in the crate.

"Where shall we take it?" asked Mr Angel.

"Depends what it is," said Laura. "Is it an indoor or outdoor prize?"

"Hmm," said Mr Angel. "Good question. I'd say both. But I'd suggest that as this is the young lady's, we should take it to her bedroom."

Lisi's bedroom was upstairs. The three men took it

up between them and dropped it off in the only free corner of Lisi's room.

"I was going to come and have a word with you in the morning," said Adam.

"Were you?" said Mr Angel. "Well, no need. A promise is a promise and a prize is a prize. Well done Lisi. Use it well."

"What is it?" Lisi asked, staring at the giant box, now resting shyly in the corner of her room.

"You'll find out in just a few minutes, I would think," said Mr Angel, "unless you want to sleep and wait till morning?"

Sleep was out of the question, but Mr Angel and his couriers refused to hang about. They said they had business to attend to.

"At midnight?" asked Adam.

"Twenty-four seven," was the reply.

They refused teas and especially refused a tip, leaving Lisi and her foster parents rather bemused.

"If the neighbours see this," said Laura, "they'll probably report us to the police."

They all felt a touch embarrassed at being so quick to doubt and to anger, but then it was an odd thing, just about the oddest thing they could imagine.

Effem, Effdee and Lisi stood in Lisi's room, staring at the crate.

"This is weird," said Laura.

"Truly weird," said Adam.

Lisi didn't say anything but stared at the crate, wide awake at this unearthly hour, not sure what to do next. Adam said the most obvious thing, which was, "I think we should open it, Lisi."

The crate was soundly built and they needed a screwdriver to release the sides. Lisi did this, then removed some protective foam to reveal the most stunning, puzzling piece of furniture, a crystal cabinet with two glittering front doors which caught and reflected light at every angle. It was like looking at a rainbow squished into a giant cube.

"This is definitely not normal," said Effem. "Do you think it's safe?"

Adam couldn't see why the manager should want to do them harm. Lisi stood in front of it and put her hands on the top.

"It's beautiful!" she said. "And warm! Feel it!"

Laura and Adam laid their hands on the cabinet. It was comfortingly, if unexpectedly, warm.

Studiously, full of unspoken expectations, Lisi pulled the doors open.

There were drawers, twenty-one of the them, all neatly numbered with semi-circular handles. In the centre was a recess in which a magnificent prism sparkled with light and colour. Above the drawers was a long, separate drawer labelled 'Instructions' and at the top was a rectangular plate fixed to the crystal on which were engraved these words:

The Cabinet of Wonders

"The what?" said Adam. "Well, when in doubt, always read the instructions."

Lisi pulled open the top drawer which slid out so smoothly she felt no resistance at all, and it didn't make the slightest sound.

Inside was a book, about the size of a scrapbook, a cleverly bound volume with "The Cabinet of Wonders" written in copperplate on the front and "Instruction Manual" beneath.

Lisi carefully opened it and read these words to her foster parents impatiently peering over her shoulder:

For you who have such troubles seen,
For you who through a war have been,
I am your prize, a mystery,
A doorway through to history.

Lay my bricks with utmost care,
Follow every rule and dare
Not cut a corner, miss a line,
Miss this chance to tangle time.

I'll come to life, I can, I shall,
Though it's for you to work out how
To meet one who has gone before
And left their mark for evermore.

One whose world was blinding light
Of reason, truth and passing night.
I'll take you where you'll fear to tread
But bring you safe back home to bed.

I'll give you hope where you have none,
And let you see what can be done.
So wisely work with words and numbers
Through this Cabinet of Wonders.

Lisi stopped reading and looked at Effem and Effdee.

"Did you understand?" she asked.

"It's a bit olde worlde," said Laura. "A kit of some kind, for making things. Sounds rather fanciful, don't you think, Adam?"

Adam didn't know what to make of it.

"Open a drawer, Lisi," he said.

Lisi gently slid open one of the drawers. It moved like silk on skin, soundlessly and smoothly. Inside were rows of ivory bricks, very small and very neatly laid out. Lisi picked one up and inspected it. It had a nice feel, not like cheap plastic but solid and weighty. Someone had taken a good deal of care making it.

"Oh, look," she said, "there's writing on it."

They checked a few other bricks. They each had engravings with letters and digits.

"It must be some kind of identification," said Adam, "so you can tell which brick goes where. Check the instruction book, Lisi."

Every page had information about the different bricks and what they could be used for, except the middle two pages which, oddly, were completely empty. Even more oddly, there was nothing to make.

"Definitely something to think about," said Adam scratching his head.

There must have been thousands of different bricks with tiny letters and numbers engraved onto one side and the manual showed each of them, but how you would actually build anything was a mystery.

Lisi opened each drawer in turn and stared at the bricks, taking one or two out, inspecting them, then putting them back. If she made a mistake and put it in the wrong place, the brick glowed red.

"Clever," whispered Adam, impressed.

When Lisi had looked into each drawer, she turned her attention to the prism in the centre of the cabinet. It was such a cheery thing to look at with colours spilling from its heart as if it was bursting with joy. Carefully, she took it out and held it in the palms of her hands. It was perfect, not a blemish on any of its faces, and the colours inside were hypnotic. When she moved it even slightly, the colours shifted as if they were dancing. And when she peered deep inside, she was sure she could see something beyond light and colour, something solid and real, but that was probably her imagination. They admired it for quite a while until Adam noticed that the glow in the main cabinet had begun to dull slightly.

"The prism might be a battery," he said. "Put it back and see, Lisi."

She did so and the cabinet appeared to buck itself up. The faint glow returned and there was even a distant sound, like the humming of bees a long way away.

"What should I do with it?" Lisi asked.

There was nothing in the book to follow, just information about each brick, like "A193: this is good for supporting windows," and "C2071: this is good for doors" and "P8342: use this for roofing."

"Good grief," said Adam, "you'd have to be a genius to make anything from this."

Now Lisi might or might not have been a genius, but she was certainly bright, and despite the mystery of the cabinet, it made more sense to her than it did to Effem and Effdee. They weren't sure what they'd expected, but it wasn't this. Lisi was delighted. She'd seen so much destroyed in her life, here was a chance to find out how to build things instead of knocking them down.

"What happens now?" Adam asked.

"Now we should all sleep," said Laura. "At least you don't have to drive back to the arcade and have an argument with the manager."

Adam was grateful for that, but he would have done anything for Lisi who was the most precious thing in his and Laura's world. They kissed her goodnight, took one last look at the new arrival then turned off the light and closed the bedroom door.

The room should have been dark, but the cabinet gave out a pale, relaxing glow.

Lay my bricks with utmost care,
Follow every rule and dare
Not cut a corner...

Lisi rolled the words over in her mind and promised she would follow every rule, but just where were they?

I'll come to life, I can, I shall...

She believed it. She trusted this peculiar, astonishingly beautiful cabinet. She didn't think it would let her down or pose her a puzzle that she couldn't solve.

Miss this chance to tangle time.

What did this mean? Was there some kind of magic in the bricks? If anyone at all had lost hope, she should have lost hers. She'd seen more than most girls her age and been through more than many grown-ups would

25

have been through in a lifetime, but a part of her refused to believe the worst. She felt that there might well be magic in the little bricks, but it was up to her to understand how to cast the spell.

She hadn't felt like this for a long while, full of expectation and ideas, and that was a good thing. She didn't want to close her eyes, unwilling to shut out the crystal cabinet, but it too must have been tired because slowly the glow faded, the room grew dark and Lisi slept.

4. Invisible Ink

Lisi spent the next week studying the manual, admiring the cabinet and wondering what to do with it. Ideas began trickling into her mind but she was a little apprehensive in case the whole kit and caboodle was nothing but a white elephant. What if she really, really believed that a model could come to life, and it didn't? How bad would that be!

She would take out a couple of bricks, hold them together and feel them stick, like magnets, even though they weren't made of metal. Something connected them, but she didn't know what. Effdee suggested that they had a tiny magnetic core, which was possible, but she was hardly going to bash one open to check.

They were the most intricately made bricks, each one with a little life of its own, she felt. She believed that losing one would be like losing a word from a sentence or a character from a story so that the rest of it would fall apart.

As for the prism, every night, she cradled it in her hands, looking deep into its heart. She hoped that one day she might see something magical, but even if she didn't, it was comforting just to hold it. There was no reason to think it could perform magic, but it was still a lovely thing. Sometimes, if light caught it at the right angle, rays of colour flashed from it in gorgeous bands, but always it felt powerful, as if full of hidden energy.

She didn't tell anyone at school. Ever since she'd started there a few months earlier, she'd been too locked away inside herself to make friends. One boy, Laszlo, helped her out when she seemed lost, but school was generally too noisy, chaotic and scary to make friends and feel comfortable. If she'd told any of her classmates or showed them the bricks or the prism, well... there would have been mayhem. Everyone would know, everyone would want to see it and that didn't seem right. This was her prize and her present and it meant something special, only she wasn't sure what yet. If she'd won a bicycle or a television then she might have let on, but this was different. Something inside told her to keep it secret, at least for a while.

She began experimenting, putting bricks together without checking the manual, trying to remember what it said about each type of brick. Nothing looked like what it was supposed to look like, but this didn't matter too much because she was practising, growing familiar with the many different shapes.

They half expected Mr Angel from the arcade to call and say that their time was up, that the cabinet was only on loan and had to be taken back, but they didn't hear from him. Lisi wondered whether she should ask Effdee to call him instead and see if she was doing anything wrong because the kit wasn't doing what it said it would on the tin, but she didn't. Patience, that was the thing. She remembered her mother telling her that a long time ago, and Effem said the same thing, that 'patience is a virtue', so she dabbled at it and never got tired of the dabbling.

The cabinet seemed to give Lisi's bedroom a warmth

it hadn't had before. Without it, the room would have felt empty. It had quickly become part and parcel of her bedroom furniture but had a place of honour. She never put her dirty clothes on it or left books or toys on top of it, that would have been wrong. It was special, even though it sat there for quite a few weeks before showing just how special it was.

The time was nine at night and Lisi was laying on her bed, leafing through the instruction manual. She'd become familiar with all the different brick shapes and felt she knew their identification numbers off by heart. For some reason, she stopped at the two empty centre pages. She'd flipped over them many times in the weeks since the cabinet had been delivered but didn't take any notice. She thought they might be for notes or even a printing error but there was nothing to look at so she didn't look.

Until now.

What did the poem say...

I'll come to life, I can, I shall,
Though it's for you to work out how

That's what it said, but what did it mean? She'd been trying for weeks. Perhaps she wasn't clever enough. She had to look at things in a different way with different eyes, but how could you look at the world with different eyes? You only had one pair and they always saw the same thing. This is why she didn't talk much to people, because they hurt each other, and it didn't matter how she looked, that's what she'd seen and learned, and so it had to be true.

She touched the centre page and brushed her forefinger over it, not for any reason that she could explain. She just did it.

Something happened. She wasn't sure what, or why, but she was sure that she saw something.

She held the book up to the light from her bedside table. Nothing. Then she held it up to the main bedroom light. Still nothing. She put it back on her bed and stroked her finger gently across the page.

"Come on," she whispered, "do it again!"

Something appeared. Writing!

Yes, definitely, a few faint lines of writing.

And a picture!

Very faint indeed, but there, on the left page!

She stroked the page as she stroked her smartphone and the writing became deeper. Too gentle and nothing happened, too hard and the image faded, so she was very careful...

Knock, knock.

"Lisi? Are you okay?" Laura opened the door and looked at Lisi who was sitting on her bed like a statue. "Lisi?"

Lisi looked up.

"It's working!" she said. "I made it work."

"Did you sweetie?" said Laura, going over to look. "Where?"

"Here," said Lisi, showing Effem what she'd been doing. The pages were empty. "There was writing here!" she said. "I made it happen!"

"I'm sure you did," said Laura, believing that Lisi was imagining things, "but time to sleep now."

Lisi hadn't imagined it at all. There'd been

something there and it had vanished when Laura opened the door.

"Would you like some chocolate?" Laura asked. "It's eleven o'clock. You should be asleep."

Eleven! Eleven? But she'd started looking at the book at nine o'clock, just a few minutes ago! How could it be eleven?

She didn't want chocolate so Laura put the manual back in the drawer, closed the cabinet doors and told Lisi to close her eyes.

As soon as Laura had gone, Lisi switched on her pen torch, tiptoed back to the cabinet, opened the doors, pulled out the instruction book and turned to the centre pages.

Empty.

She settled herself down on the floor with the book in her lap and gently rubbed her fingertip over the pages. Slowly, slowly, line by line and shade by shade, things began to appear. If she moved her hand too fast then nothing happened, and if she pressed too heavily then the images faded, but if she pressed just right and moved at just the right speed then not only words but coloured diagrams formed...

And moved!

It was like a state-of-the art touch screen but made of paper, or something that looked very much like paper.

When the two pages were full, Lisi studied her handiwork.

She was looking at a spectacular arch glowing with every colour of the rainbow. Around it were instructions numbered 1 to 10 and then, if she slid her forefinger down, the instructions grew from 11 to 20, then 21 to

30, then... well, she didn't get to the end. How could there be so many instructions? She read one. It told her which brick to choose and where to put it. And there were little diagrams which appeared and disappeared if she ran her finger along the lines.

She stared at the rainbow arch. It was the most wonderful thing, so simple and so beautiful. She just had to make it! But she daren't start it now because it was late and Effem and Effdee would know she wasn't sleeping. She would have to leave it to the morning or the weekend when she had time. Only supposing that it all disappeared and wouldn't come back? That would be terrible, unbearable. It had taken her weeks to get this far and now she'd discovered the secret of the instruction manual it would be beyond cruel if it all vanished.

She closed the book but, a moment later, opened it again. The picture and instructions were still there! Thank goodness for that. She had another look at the arch, moved it around with her finger and saw that she could rotate it and zoom in and zoom out. The more she looked the more she thought how hard it would be to build. Every part of the arch was numbered and she remembered the instructions,

Lay my bricks with utmost care,
Follow every rule and dare
Not cut a corner, miss a line,
Miss this chance to tangle time.

She knew what she had to do, and saw exactly what it would look like, but seeing it in the book was one thing, making it was another. How big would it be? Would it fit into her bedroom? What would Effdee and Effem say? And would it... could it... come to life? How could an arch come to life? She had so many questions but she was feeling overwhelmingly tired. She closed the book, put it back into the cabinet, shut the doors and climbed into bed. In her mind's eye, all she could see was the beautiful arch, but even that faded as she drifted off to sleep.

5. Building Works

Lisi couldn't concentrate at school. She did her best, as she always did, but she kept thinking of what she'd discovered. That morning, the very first thing she did was to check the manual and make sure the arch and the instructions were still there. Her heart was in her mouth when she opened the book, fearing that it had all been imagined, but there it was! Such a relief.

Laszlo said to her that she looked different but he couldn't say how. Lisi wanted to tell him about the cabinet and the book and the arch. Why shouldn't she? She never told anyone anything and it often felt like all her secret life would explode inside her. Laszlo was a good boy and always took her side if anyone was nasty to her, which they sometimes were because she was different.

She said nothing because she didn't know how to put everything that was in her heart into words. Effem and Effdee had taken her to a doctor who would have listened but Lisi wouldn't talk to her. When the time, the place and the person were right, she might open up, but not before. Meanwhile, she lived inside a tight little prison, only now it seemed a little less tight and a little less little!

She told Effem and Effdee that she'd decided to make something, but they weren't to look.

"Why not?" asked Laura?

"I'll show you when it's done," said Lisi, "but it may take a long time."

"What, a day, two days, a week?" said Adam.

"Don't know," said Lisi. "It will be a surprise."

Laura and Adam wondered what was going on but they trusted Lisi and said they wouldn't go in to look until she said she was ready.

That evening she cleared a space on the floor, opened the instruction book at the centre pages and touched the first line. Little popups appeared with brick numbers and an illustration showing her how to begin.

So she began.

"Remember," a popup said, "the journey of a thousand miles begins with a single step."

A thousand miles seemed like a long way but she got the message - patience, and she was a patient girl.

She had to make a single base about a metre long and thirty centimetres wide. This took dozens of bricks, but as the cabinet held about a zillion, this wasn't a problem. There were gaps in the base where the main arch was going to be supported and special corner bricks which rounded off the edges. It took her three nights to complete the base. She might have finished sooner but she also had to keep the rest of her life in order, including homework and quality time with Effdee and Effem who were curious to know what she was doing but kept their promise not to peek.

At the weekend she got moving with the lower sides of the arch. She was instructed to move at the same level for both the left and right sides, keeping them at the same height, so she built one row on the left, another on the right, checking each time that she was using the right bricks. If she ignored the instructions the wrong brick wouldn't stay in place. It was like trying to push two identical magnetic poles together, it couldn't be done. If she forced it, the brick would glow red and look quite angry, for a brick, so there was no choice but to follow the instructions.

The sides were smooth and repetitive but it took her a weekend to build them, each about one metre fifty high. She would sometimes sit back and admire the growing structure as if she were a proper builder building houses and offices and bridges and everything that made up the world. This was an especially good feeling as she remembered how terribly easy it was to destroy the same things – a single moment and all was gone. She'd seen it, she knew it, but she'd never built anything. This was the first time and she realised how much effort it took.

She'd seen arches before but it hadn't occurred to her how clever they were. She'd certainly not thought about how you build one, but now she had to, and it was interesting. After all, you couldn't start at the top and work down, of course, nor could you do one side at a time and work around. What you had to do was build both sides evenly together until they met, but you had to be careful not to rush otherwise the overhang might collapse.

Lisi scrolled her finger down the list of things to do and the manual showed her how to make the curved bits strong as they began to close in on each other. Tricky. There were moments when Lisi thought the whole thing looked shaky but she'd followed the instructions to the letter and each day the curved sides grew closer together. When she was out and about, she took more notice of the men and women working on the roads and building sites. She watched them carefully, seeing how they measured everything, never rushing, always so focused. A foreman at one of these sites saw Lisi staring and had a chat with her, telling her about the different types of bricks and cement and how they made sure everything fitted neatly. Lisi had a million questions, but three or four had to do for the time being. She was desperate to tell what she was building but the foreman probably wouldn't have believed her. If you told someone you were building a rainbow arch in your bedroom they were bound not to believe you.

That night she worked even harder, making sure each level of brick was secure and in place. As ever, if she made a mistake or hurried, the brick would glow red and refuse to be placed. Without these warnings it would have been easy to make a mistake and not notice until the whole thing collapsed.

She reached a point where there were only about ten centimetres between the growing curves which formed the top of the arch. It had taken her two weeks to get there, and Effem and Effdee had kept their word and never looked. They were intrigued, of course, and it was all they could do not to ask or peek inside.

In a way, Lisi didn't want to finish. It had been absorbing following the instructions and seeing the arch grow. It was taller than her by a few centimetres and she often walked underneath it, checking that each and every brick was secure. She pretended to be a building site foreman, giving instructions to her workers, do this, do that.

She was ninety-nine point nine percent sure that nothing would happen but couldn't dispel a tiny speck of belief deep down inside. Most likely though, she'd put the final brick in place, waiting for the arch to come to life, but it would just stand there, impressive but silent.

Did it matter, she asked herself? She would be disappointed, of course, because the instructions clearly said that it would come to life, but on the other hand, not many other girls her age had built such a thing. It was an achievement. So she prepared herself for it to be no more than it was. And anyway, what did it mean, "come to life"? Buildings were never alive. It wouldn't become a pair of legs and walk away, would it? That would be silly.

Three weeks after she'd started she had just ten bricks left. The arch had already come together at the top, but it wasn't complete. The final ten bricks had to be put in place and Lisi wanted this to be a special occasion. She cleaned her room and made it even tidier than usual. She closed the cabinet doors, put the ten final bricks on top then sat on her bed and had a good, long ponder.

The arch was white because the bricks were white, so the colourful rainbow drawing in the instruction manual wasn't accurate. She'd known this all the time. You couldn't make a white wall from brown bricks and you couldn't make a rainbow arch from white bricks, unless you painted them, and that was cheating.

It was a splendid thing. More than splendid, it was astonishing, so much so that Lisi decided this was the moment to share it with Effem and Effdee. On Sunday evening after supper she said to her foster parents, "Laura and Adam thank you for being so patient. You can come up to my room now, if you want. I will show you what I've been doing."

They stared at her, once again taken by their step-daughter's kindness, good manners and polite invitation. It had been a month since she asked them not to enter her bedroom and they'd kept their word.

"Is it finished, whatever you've built, sweetie?" asked Effem.

"Almost," said Lisi. "A few more bricks, but I know where they go and I want you to be there when it's done."

They had no idea what 'it' was, but they were delighted that Lisi trusted them enough to let them in on the secret at last. Months past, they hadn't been sure whether adoption would work out. Lisi was a silent girl who had been through a terrible ordeal and they were warned that she might be difficult. Well, she hadn't been difficult at all, she'd been brilliant, just quiet, nursing her own hurt and pain. This was the first time they felt she was offering them something special, something of herself.

Even so, they weren't prepared for what they saw. They hadn't a clue what to expect but they probably imagined something small, childish and quaint. They definitely didn't expect a beautiful ivory arch in the centre of Lisi's bedroom, three quarters of the way to the ceiling and looking like something which might have been buit by Leonardo da Vinci.

"Good grief, Lisi!" exclaimed Adam. "Did you make this?"

She had made it.

Laura stared open mouthed. She walked around it, inspected it, stroked it and walked underneath it.

"Lisi, it's... it's astonishing! We should tell the newspapers to come and see. They'll take a picture and..."

"No!" said Lisi firmly. "Just you two and me, and maybe a friend one day, but nobody else."

"Lisi," said Laura, "that would be such a pity. This is extraordinary!"

"I'll show you," said Lisi, and she took one of the ten pieces on top of the cabinet, stood on a chair and locked it into place on top of the arch. Then she took another and another and locked them into place. She didn't show them the way the bricks glowed red if she got things wrong, nor the way the instruction manual worked like a top of the range tablet, but she proved to them that she knew what she was doing.

Nine pieces in place, one piece left. She stood on the chair, but did nothing.

"Is that the last?" asked Adam.

Lisi nodded, twiddling the brick between her thumb and forefinger.

"Go on Lisi," said Laura, "then you can come down and admire your work. It's fabulous."

Lisi hesitated. If she hadn't asked Effem and Effdee to come and look then the magic might feel freer to show itself, but with them staring at her and the arch, there was no way anything out of the ordinary would happen. But then again, if she was alone and nothing happened, there would be no lame excuses and she would know for certain that it offered nothing more.

So nothing to lose.

She lifted her arm, stretched, placed the final ivory brick into position and stepped down.

Laura put her arm around Lisi's shoulder and said, "It's the most wonderful thing I've ever seen, Lisi! I don't know how you did it. Not many children your age could do such a thing. I doubt many adults could do it either."

Lisi looked at the arch and waited, hoping, half-hoping, a quarter hoping...

Nothing.

Of course nothing happened! What did she expect? She mustn't be so silly. You can't believe everything you read, not even in the instruction manual of strange jackpot prizes - *especially* in the instruction manual of strange jackpot prizes. It was just words. Anyone could write words. You can say what you like, lie as much as you like, no one knows until the promises don't come true. No point being disappointed.

"I thought something might happen," she whispered, half to herself, half to Effem and Effdee.

"Look at it, Lisi. Don't you think there's wonder in what you've made here? You should be so proud."

The arch dominated Lisi's bedroom and despite it being just plain and white there was something about it that was mysterious, but whatever 'it' was, you couldn't give it a name. Adam walked around it, touched it, bowed as he passed underneath and said, "Lisi, this is stunning! How talented you are! Are you sure you don't want us to call the papers or the television news? They'd love to see it."

Lisi shook her head. She didn't want anyone else to

know. This was private and confidential, not for any particular reason, just that she wanted it that way.

Her foster parents were so fascinated, they could have stayed and stared for hours in admiration. They felt closer to Lisi than ever before and didn't want to lose the moment, but eventually they had to let it go and let her get ready for bed.

After all the goodnights, Lisi lay wrapped in her comfy duvet, staring through the dark at the pale glow of the arch. Minutes passed, minutes that seemed to stretch into dream time. She wasn't sure if she'd dropped off to sleep and woken again or had been laying awake all the time but something caught her attention - a sound, like a faint and distant humming.

She opened her eyes, or thought she did, because what she saw couldn't be real.

The arch was no longer white. All the colours of the rainbow raced through it, alive with light, and through this shimmering, glimmering rainbow, Lisi saw something that took her breath away.

5. An Unhappy Boy

It took a few moments for Lisi to register what she was seeing, blinking to make sure she was awake, but once she'd convinced herself, she sat up in bed, rubbing her eyes to make the vision clearer.

She was looking at a room, old-fashioned and dreary with a four poster bed in the corner, a table and chair in the middle, some heavy looking books in heavy looking bookcases and a single window with a thick velvet curtain drawn closed. She stood, waited, then tiptoed towards the arch. The image became crystal clear. She held her breath. A candle in a fancy candlestick stood in the centre of the table, unlit. A tiny light glowed from a wick lantern on the mantelpiece over a dead fireplace.

A boy was tossing and turning in the bed. He was also crying, and occasionally bashing his pillow with tight fists. Startlingly fast, he sat up and seemed to look straight into Lisi's eyes. Her mouth dropped open in surprise and she could hear her heart beat faster. She put her hand to her mouth to stop any sound escaping as she tried to calm herself. Could he see her? He seemed to be looking directly at her and she saw every tear stain on his face. What was the matter with him? Was he in pain? Should she call Effem to come and help? Where was his mother? What should she do?

The boy rubbed his eyes just as she'd rubbed hers, but then he looked away. If he'd seen her, then he must have thought it was a dream because he made no move towards her nor said a word.

His face was dark and broody and the most miserable Lisi had ever seen. She knew she was a serious girl but this boy looked like he had the weight of the world on his shoulders.

He sat up and let his legs dangle over the edge of the impressive bed, four posts holding up rich maroon drapes and lace curtains, one of which was drawn back allowing Lisi to see him.

He wasn't wearing pyjamas but a nightdress like a girl might have worn. He kicked his legs back and forward and muttered to himself athough Lisi couldn't hear what he was saying. She couldn't hear anything. If this was a TV picture it had the sound turned down.

He stood up and remained perfectly still, staring at the floor for minutes on end. Lisi settled down a little but still wasn't sure what to do. She was so close that if she took just a few steps she would be in the room with him. She stood still, waiting and watching.

The boy remained motionless, staring at the floor as if it was the most interesting floor in the world. After an excruciatingly long while he walked over to the window and drew open one of the curtains.

It was dark outside but the moon was half full and the sky was peppered with stars. Lisi could see precious little evidence of night life, no city lights, just the moon and starlight. The boy stared at them as intently as he had stared at the floor and this appeared to calm him down a little.

Lisi lost track of how long the unhappy boy stood staring out of the window and how long she stood by the arch staring at him. She was fascinated not just by the impossibility of what was happening but by the boy's face. She'd only ever seen one other face so absorbed, so creased with worry and so sad – that was hers when she looked into a mirror. Was the same thing troubling him that troubled her? She was so tempted to ask, but if she stepped into the room she might not be able to step back. She would wait a minute and see.

The boy turned away suddenly and looked directly at Lisi again, or at least he seemed to. She held her breath, waiting for him to ask who she was and what she was doing in his room but he said nothing.

He moved to the table in the centre of the room and pulled out the chair. He didn't do it gently but scraped the floor and seemed ready to pick the chair up and throw it through the window. He was evidently in a foul mood.

He opened a book on the desk and began reading. Lisi couldn't see what the book was about but it was three times as big as any book she'd ever seen and twice as thick. The cover was stiff and brown and looked like it weighed a ton. The boy, his face focused like a laser, read avidly, turning the pages slowly and muttering the words as he read them. Lisi would have given anything to know what he was reading but she couldn't see. She doubted it was anything easy. Apart from looking severe and angry in the extreme, the boy also looked frighteningly clever.

He picked up a pen, not a biro or felt tip or even a fancy expensive pen but a feather quill which he dipped every now and again into a small bottle of ink. He also picked up a piece of paper, only this wasn't normal paper either, it was thick and weighty, more like parchment than the paper Lisi used at school.

When he'd done writing, he picked up the parchment and read what he'd written. Lisi saw some numbers and letters but couldn't make sense of it and didn't have time to study it because in a flash the boy tore it into shreds and threw the pieces into a waste basket. He then kicked his bed three times and sat on the edge again, sulking madly.

Lisi wondered if she scared people as much as the boy scared her. His eyes were dark, like hers, and they were set deep and unfathomable in his head which was plastered with thick, straight black hair. For all the world, he looked like some furious apprentice magician. Lisi half expected him to take out a wand and magic her into the room, but whatever weird stuff was going on in the arch, the boy was firmly rooted in his own real and un-magical room.

There was a knock on the door. Lisi turned, but this was not her door, it was the door in the boy's bedroom. It was faint and distant but she'd actually heard it! The door in the room opened and an old lady stood there, looking at the boy sitting on the edge of his bed, swinging his legs, glum bordering on misery.

He turned towards her but no smiles were exchanged. In fact he glared at her as though she were his mortal enemy but she took no notice, came in and hurried him into bed. Words were exchanged and although Lisi couldn't hear them, they didn't seem to be words of great friendliness.

The old lady tucked him up then leaned over to kiss him but he turned away to face Lisi who saw the bitterness in his eyes. Was she a witch keeping him prisoner, like Hansel and Gretel? Was she fattening him up to eat him? What was going on?

The old lady left and immediately the boy jumped out of bed and stood there, his face screwed up in fierce concentration, then suddenly started banging his fists against his head in sheer frustration. Lisi almost cried out for him to stop but he stopped all by himself and calmed himself.

He hesitated, looked around, then knelt down beneath the bed, searching for something. A few moments later he came up holding a metal tin, locked with an impressively large key. Was this a treasure chest full of gold? Lisi watched, spellbound.

The unhappy boy, unhappier than ever, put the tin on the table, turned the key and opened the lid. There was no gold inside, nor any obvious treasure, but the boy still handled whatever it was with care.

He took out what Lisi at first thought might be a photograph, but it wasn't. It was a miniature painting. Lisi guessed that wherever and whenever this was, it was too early for photographs. She could see a woman's face, young, handsome, happy. The boy kissed it, looked at it some more, then laid it on the table and started pounding it with his fist.

Was he mad, Lisi wondered? She didn't understand this strange behaviour.

After a few moments he settled himself then rummaged around inside the tin again, taking out a small glass lens. He moved to the window, holding the lens up to the moon. A change seemed to come over him. His fury subsided and a calmness spread across his face. Lisi breathed a sigh of relief. She'd thought he was about to explode but this little glass trinket worked a peculiar, peace-giving spell on him.

He looked through it, holding it at arm's length for a while, then slowly moving it back and forth, apparently seeing the difference it made to the moon and stars in the night sky.

He glanced at the door, seemed satisfied that the old lady wasn't coming back and took a taper from the tin over to the lantern on the mantelpiece above the extinguished fire. The lantern flame was very small but the boy dipped the taper into it and held it there until it caught alight, then he shut the lantern door and carried the flickering taper to the candle on the table.

Very gently he lit the candle and stared at it. Then he held the glass lens in front and moved it towards and away from the flame, peering through the glass the whole time.

Lisi almost laughed at the boy's face. It had gone from fury to funny in a few seconds. He was no longer a ferocious, ill tempered monster but a little boy fascinated by a candle flame.

His eyes were remarkably still. Lisi felt almost hypnotised by them. The boy took up his pen and another sheet of parchment and, oh so carefully, started to draw what he saw. Lisi couldn't see the drawing but she knew what he was doing. He studied part of the flame, drew it, checked the drawing then went back to the flame. He concentrated intently, oblivious to everything else. Was he an artist? What did he find so intriguing about a simple flame?

Time seemed to move around Lisi in slow motion.

She couldn't tell how long she'd been standing there, but she didn't want to leave. This was the most bizarre, exciting, inexplicable, riveting vision and she desperately wanted to know who the boy was and why he was being held prisoner in that room – if that was what was happening. And of course she wanted to know why he was so furious one minute, so calm and intent the next, almost as if he were two people wrapped into one.

Eventually, he finished drawing and held up the parchment, away from Lisi so that she couldn't see what he'd drawn. He studied it but from his expression Lisi couldn't tell whether he was pleased with his efforts or not. He settled down again and started some more writing, only this time he didn't keep looking at the candle or the lens. He seemed to be working from somewhere deep inside. Lisi was more curious than ever to know what he was doing but she couldn't see. A few times she was tempted to step forward and show herself but she guessed that the poor boy would be shocked out of his skin so she held back.

He finished whatever he was doing, sat back and looked fairly satisfied. He packed up the tin, put it back under the bed, snuffed out the candle and climbed into bed. He tossed and turned a couple of times, then lay still.

Lisi was wide awake. She had no idea how long she'd been standing there and she couldn't just go back to bed. She had to know if this was real and she wanted to see what he'd been drawing. Summoning up all her courage, she took a step forward.

Whatever happened, it happened so fast that she had

no time to change her mind. She felt as if she'd walked through a wall of feathers. Her skin tickled all over and for a moment she was giddy, but it faded as she stepped into the olde worlde room.

Was this the most foolish thing she had ever done? She panicked and looked behind her, afraid that she had passed through a one-way passage into the past, but there was her bedroom, quivering in the archway. Had the boy seen this? How had he not seen it?

She took a step forward and the bedroom vanished.

Lisi's heart missed a beat.

All she could see was a panelled wooden wall with five arches made of curved wood. The middle one was directly in front of her. She moved towards it and immediately saw her bedroom again, took a step back and it disappeared, forward and it reappeared.

She turned, silent as the night, and took in the atmosphere of the room. The boy was fast asleep. If she'd made any noise, he hadn't heard her. He was snoring, facing the wall away from Lisi. She stood still, turning her head to look at every detail. It was different to watching it from behind the archway. This was real. It felt real, smelt real and sounded real with the boy's funny snoring and some occasional house sounds, a creak here and a tap there, the kinds of sounds all houses make at night.

Lisi tiptoed over to the table, watching the boy, ready to race back to the arch if he woke up or the old lady returned, but the boy slept on and the door remained closed.

On the table was the parchment with a wonderful drawing of the candle, but not just a drawing; there were arrows next to parts of the flame and writing next to the arrows, like little labels. It was as if the boy was trying to understand why the flame took that particular shape and why it glowed with those particular colours. Lisi would never ever have thought of doing this. To her, a flame was a flame and nothing to get excited about, but evidently the boy had a more curious mind. Lisi couldn't read everything he'd written because the spelling was odd and there were smudges where the ink had run, but she knew for sure what he'd been trying to do. She was impressed.

She tiptoed towards the window and stood where she'd seen the boy stand just a little while earlier. The moon was the very same moon she saw back home. It wasn't green and there weren't two of them. She could even see the shadows of the man in the moon. And though she was no expert on stars, there was nothing to suggest these weren't the same stars she saw through her own bedroom window at night.

But the Earth was different. It was probably still Earth, but the sea of lights that lit up the modern world was gone. This was almost pure darkness, and not because they were in the middle of nowhere. Lisi could see the shadows of houses, only they were dark, and the darkness spread far and wide. There wasn't an electric light in sight. Any breaks in the darkness, apart from the lights in the night sky, came from a few flickering candles in distant windows.

On one of the walls were two large and very grand paintings, a man and a woman. Both looked as if they owned the world, staring out confidently into the room. The man wore a smart but old fashioned suit with a crinkly cravat and the woman a flouncy dress which must have been tricky to put on. Were these the boy's parents, Lisi wondered? Who, then, was the old lady she'd seen hurry him into bed?

Lisi turned to look at the sleeping boy. He was safely in dreamland, snoring slightly. Lisi knelt down beneath the bed and took out the tin. She felt like a thief, but she didn't intend to steal anything, just to look. She put it on the table. It was a wonderfully decorated tin, not the kind of plain old thing in which Effem kept biscuits and cakes. This had various colourful pictures on it and was quite heavy. She turned the key.

Inside was a jumble of bric-a-brac. Lisi took out the lens. It was strange to touch what she'd seen the boy use but she held it carefully and looked through it. The convex glass distorted whatever she looked at. She took it to the window and saw the moon and stars as the boy had seen them, close up but twisted and fuzzy. She peered at the sleeping boy through the lens and he became a muddle of colours and shapes.

The sketch was definitely the same lady as the one in the painting, cleverly drawn. There was a wooden puzzle, a ring, a concave lens, an abacus, quite a few coins and a pocket watch. Lisi held the pocket watch in her hand. It was silver and circular with detailed engravings on the cover and a button on the top. She pressed it and it clicked open. Inside was the watch face with just one hand – the other had apparently broken off. There was no ticking.

Lisi started to feel guilty nosing through the tin like that. She wasn't stealing, but it was the unhappy boy's private property so she put everything back and slid the tin under the bed.

She sat at the table and opened the book he'd been reading. She was expecting fairy tales or stories but it was a book about money. This is what she thought at first, but in fact it was about making money – not like banks and savings and business she heard about on television a hundred times a day, but actually how to *make* money, with metals and furnaces and things like that. What kind of head did this strange boy have to want to see how money was made?

Lisi turned the pages and saw coins from many different times in history with detailed explanations about how they'd been forged, their proportions of silver, gold, copper and other metals, how hot to heat the furnaces, how to cool the metal and so on. Hundreds of pages about making money! She closed it, ever more intrigued by the sleeping boy locked away in this solitary, musty old room.

She inspected some of the books in the bookcases. None of them were story books. They were all to do with weird grown up subjects and even some on arithmetic, but not the kind of National Curriculum arithmetic she learned at school. She took out one volume which weighed as much as a baby elephant and inside were diagrams of triangles and circles with all kinds of explanations. It was written by someone called Euclid.

She was beginning to think that the boy wasn't a boy at all, more that he was a wise old man trapped in a boy's body. She was thinking many thoughts when she realized that something had changed. For a moment she wasn't sure what it was, but she felt that the atmosphere in the room was different. Why?

Then she realized.

No more snoring!

The room was absolutely quiet. More than that, she felt another presence, not fast asleep but wide awake. She spun round and froze. The unhappy boy was sitting up in bed, wide awake, his dark eyes, now almost the size of saucepans, fixed on her, fearful and astonished.

6. Isaac

Lisi's first reaction was to run, but when she looked at the arch in the wooden panels, all she saw was just that, a wooden panelled archway. If her bedroom was still there, beyond the archway, she couldn't see it. Besides, he was just a boy, and a miserable one at that. She didn't want to feel afraid or to show fear.

"Who are you? What do you want? How did you get in here?"

His voice was quivering, but so would hers be if she woke up and found a stranger nosing around in her bedroom.

"My name is Lisi. I don't want anything. And I'm not sure how I got here. It's a long story."

The boy didn't know whether the girl was a dream, a ghost or some kind of vision. He rubbed his eyes but didn't get out of bed.

"I shall call grandmother."

"You don't have to," said Lisi. "I mean, I'm not going to hurt you or steal anything. I'll go if you want."

The boy was unsure, but each passing moment he felt a little safer. The girl didn't look menacing, in fact she had a nice face. He didn't make a move to call for help.

He looked around, puzzled.

"I don't understand how you got in," he said. "The doors are locked."

"It's complicated," said Lisi.

"I'm clever," said the boy with a noticeable lack of modesty. "You can tell me. I'll understand."

"I'm sure you will," said Lisi, "but I don't understand it myself, and I'm the one who's here." She paused for a moment, then asked, "Do you read *all* these books?"

"Of course I do."

"And you study the stars with your little lens?"

"Yes, I... how did you know that? Have you been spying on me?"

Lisi hesitated. "Not on purpose, no, but it really is a long story. I saw you angry..."

"When?"

"Just before, when the old lady came in..."

"Grandmother?"

"I suppose so. And then I saw you looking through the lens and drawing and writing stuff."

"How?" said the boy. "Where were you hiding? You weren't here, I know you weren't!"

"No," said Lisi, "I wasn't. I was there," and she pointed to the wooden panel.

The boy climbed out of bed, put on a velvet dressing gown and walked to the wooden panelled archway.

"Be careful!" Lisi said, half expecting him to tumble into her bedroom, but he knocked on the wood and it seemed solid. He turned to her with a puzzled expression.

"Show me," he said.

Lisi tried not to panic. Supposing she touched the wooden panel and it was just wood, not the way back? First, the boy would call her a liar, fetch his grandmother and then, chaos. Second, that would mean her room and her world were gone, maybe forever. She approached the panel and breathed a sigh of relief when she saw her bedroom reappear beyond the arch. The boy, though, could see nothing at all.

"Well?" he said, anger rising in his voice.

"Goodbye," said Lisi, and she walked through the panel, back into her bedroom. When she turned, she could see the boy staring as if he'd really seen a ghost. Lisi might well have stayed put, leaving him with a troubling memory, but that would be unfair. The poor boy looked miserable enough, she didn't want to make things worse. She passed through the arch again into his bedroom. He backed away, bewildered.

"I'm not a ghost," said Lisi. "I'm just like you. I'm real."

"But..."

"I know, I told you, it's complicated."

The boy felt the wall again, then quite abruptly he pinched Lisi's arm.

"Ow! Don't do that!"

"I'm sorry! I'm sorry!" he sounded really apologetic. "I hate hurting things, truly! I didn't think you were solid!"

"Well I am, so don't do that again!"

She rubbed her arm, looked at him and saw that he was deeply apologetic.

"My name is Isaac," he said, inspecting the wooden panel. "This is my house."

"Why don't you get your lens out," she said, seeing that he was more interested in the wall than in her, "then you can see it close up."

"Were you looking at me all the time?" he asked.

"Not all the time, just when you couldn't sleep."

Isaac wouldn't leave the wooden panel alone.

"I don't like mysteries," he said.

"Neither do I," said Lisi, "but it is one. You see I won this prize at the arcade and the manager and two men brought it round to our house and it was this kit for making things..."

"Making what things?" asked Isaac.

"An arch, in my bedroom, honestly, and I walked through it into this room."

Although it was a fast-forward retelling of all that had happened, Isaac seemed to get the drift.

"How did you make it?" he asked.

"With bricks. There are drawers full of them, hundreds and hundreds. It took me weeks, and I had to follow every instruction carefully. If I made a mistake, then it wouldn't work."

Isaac listened attentively. He wasn't sure what to make of this tale, but the fact was, the girl was here in his bedroom and she'd just walked through a solid wooden wall and back again.

"I want to see it," he said.

"I don't think you can," said Lisi. "I mean, I would if I could but you just felt the wall and it was just a wall. It doesn't want to work for you."

Isaac tapped the panel all over. He put his ear to it and stared at it close up, but nothing altered. It remained solid wood. He gave up, looked again at Lisi, had a private think, seemed to decide that she wasn't a threat and might even be friendly, then walked to the old fireplace beneath the paintings.

"These are my parents," he said. "Only my father is... is dead."

He could hardly say the word.

"I'm sorry," said Lisi. "What happened?"

"He was ill. I never saw him," said Isaac. His voice was oddly hoarse and quiet. He found it hard to speak these words. "He died before I was born."

"That's very sad," said Lisi. "But at least you've got your mother to look after you."

Isaac's eyes flashed. Lisi felt a sudden fear, as if the boy had some madness inside him, but he seemed to be in control of himself, even if he was angry.

"I do not! She left me. She married another man and left me here with grandmother."

"Oh," said Lisi. "I'm sorry about that too. Is that why you are so unhappy?"

Isaac almost shouted, "I am **not** unhappy!" which was an odd thing to say as he was clearly as miserable as sin.

They were quiet for a moment, then Isaac said with a tinge of spite in his voice, "I suppose your mother and father are waiting for you to come back into their loving arms."

Lisi wasn't sure whether she was going to like Isaac. He seemed again to be two people wrapped in one body, one kind, one mean. She didn't answer. She never answered questions about her parents, not at school, not to her teacher, not to friends, not even to Effem and Effdee. She didn't know what to say now so she stood looking down, remembering but silent.

"I told you," said Isaac. "You don't have to say anything, I know. It's the way it is, always."

"Not always," whispered Lisi.

Isaac caught a hint of some secret in her words.

"Who is waiting for you then?" he asked.

She thought for a moment more and said, "I'll tell you when I'm ready, not because you bully me to tell."

Isaac felt a tug of remorse. It was hard for him to feel sorry for anyone else because he was so affected by his own anger and sorrow, but he sensed that this girl might well be hiding an equal measure of sadness. He held his tongue for half a minute then said, "I'm sorry. I can be rude sometimes. I don't mean to be."

He spoke like a little boy lost now, wanting and needing a friend. All the anger had evaporated. Nearly all of it, anyway.

"That's alright."

"No," said Isaac, "it isn't, but it's done now. I try to be good, I really do, but the world can be such a horrid place. Sometimes, I wonder why my mother brought me into it in the first place."

"Because she must have loved your father," said Lisi. "That's what normally happens. I don't suppose she knew he was going to die."

Isaac looked glum. He had thought about this a million times but never came to a happy conclusion. He was abandoned, that was the beginning and end of it, and no matter how you glossed it over with whys and wherefores, you couldn't come up with an agreeable reason.

"No," he whispered, "but he did die. I won't, not for a long time. Just to spite them all! I'll be old and grey and famous too! You wait and see. I'll annoy them, especially him!"

"Him who?"

"My stepfather!"

Isaac stamped the ground in anger. He was a real hothead, one minute calm and apologetic, the next an exploding volcano.

"You don't like him?"

"No, I don't like him, I hate him!"

"Why, is he nasty to you?"

Isaac's face had grown dark and glowering, but he was doing his best to fight the feelings that upset him so much. Something strange had happened, and this girl had appeared with a story of her own that was too awful to tell, he knew it, so he shouldn't go on about himself, it was just so hard not to!

"I don't want to speak of him," Isaac said. "He makes me cry."

"Yes," said Lisi, "I saw you."

Unexpectedly, Isaac suddenly smiled, an innocent, captivating smile.

"I bet you thought me a sissy!" he said.

"No," said Lisi. "I felt sorry for you. I wanted to come through and talk to you but then the old lady came in."

"Humph!" said Issac. "She always gets in the way. So you spied on me and then came in when I was asleep?"

"Yes, but you would have done the same thing. You would have been scared out of your wits if I'd pounced on you like that."

"I was scared."

"Not any more?"

"No. You seem to be... safe."

"I am safe," said Lisi. "Although..."

"What?"

"I'm not sure what I'm doing here."

That was interesting, and as Isaac liked interesting things this whole midnight adventure was fast turning into the most interesting thing that had ever happened to him. If it was true that she wasn't sure why all this had happened, then she was as lost as him and needed his good will as much as he needed hers.

"How much did you see?" he asked her.

She told him what she'd seen him do, including the writing, the drawing, staring at the stars, taking out the tin from under his bed and rummaging through his secret treasures.

"What were you writing?" she asked him.

Isaac looked sheepish, as if he was conscious of being what Lisi might have called an anorak. The boys at school hounded him for being a swat, but he couldn't help it, that's exactly what he was. He showed her the parchment with his drawings and scribbles.

"I was wondering why the flame has different colours," he said. "I was trying to calculate how hot each part of it would be."

That was impressive! There was not a snowball's chance on Mars that Lisi would ever do something like that. She would never even have thought of asking the question. And what was more, she couldn't think of anyone in her school who might have asked it – oh, except for Laszlo. He was bright and curious, but even he wouldn't understand Isaac's formulas.

Isaac explained his ideas and she listened, but he could see she didn't understand. This disappointed him, she could tell, but he was used to it. No one understood what he understood. He put the parchment in a book made from two pieces of wood bound together with cord. There were about two hundred pieces of parchment inside. He was going to close it when Lisi held his arm and asked to see. He let her, quite proud of his work, even if she wasn't going to understand it. She didn't, but she was absolutely fascinated and looked at every page.

"Did you do all this?" she asked.

He was touchingly shy about saying yes. Inside were drawings, ideas and calculations about everything, not just candles, but coins (lots about coins), the Earth and the stars (lots too about the Earth and the stars), the sun, the moon and hundreds of geometric drawings from squares to dodecahedrons, all with scribbled notes next to them.

"I like to find out why everything is the way it is. People tell me not to bother because only 'God knows' but I want to know too. Don't you?"

"Of course I do," said Lisi.

Isaac warmed to her even more. Lisi gave the book back and Isaac put it back in the bookcase alongside two similar sized volumes.

"Are they...?" Lisi began to ask.

"Yes," said Isaac. "Ever since I was seven. I keep everything, but it's not all good. I just want to understand, and I don't, not yet, but I will, one day."

Lisi thought him odder by the moment but she was beginning to like him again. He was what Effdee would call 'troubled' and 'difficult'. Lisi was similar but she doubted that she was as troubled and difficult as Isaac.

"You've seen the treasure tin?" he asked.

"Under the bed, yes. Sorry."

Lisi was embarrassed. She felt like a spy who had been caught out but Isaac accepted what had happened. He knelt down, brought out the tin again and opened it. Slowly and lovingly, he put all the treasures on the table.

"Anything I find interesting I put in here," he said. "It's almost full up so I'll need a new one soon. Sometimes I feel like I need to put the whole world inside it, but it won't fit."

He looked at Lisi with a mischievous face and she smiled. There were some other things in the box which she hadn't noticed earlier including a compass and a rolled up map. She opened the map out and recognised the world even though it was very different from maps she knew.

"Well, you have put the world inside it," she said.

"I never thought of that," he laughed, a very light and lovely laugh that was rarely heard. "Where are you from?"

Lisi pointed to a far away area, far from England, on the edge of Europe.

"I can't see my country," she said, "but it should be here."

"This is England," said Isaac. "Don't you live here?" he asked.

"Yes," she said, "but it looks different on your map. Maybe... here?"

Lisi pointed roughly to the area where she lived with Effem and Effdee.

"But that's Woolsthorpe!" said Isaac. "Right here! That can't be right. I would know you, wouldn't I?"

"I've never heard of Woolsthorpe," said Lisi. "And we don't know each other. And this map is all topsy turvy."

Neither of them, as bright as they were, and as bright as Isaac was especially, had realised the truth. Lisi might have watched a few episodes of Dr. Who but that was television. Working out something as odd as this in real life was totally different.

"The map is the best there is," said Isaac. "I don't go out much so there are many places I haven't seen. You are... different, though."

"So are you," said Lisi.

She touched the treasures and asked about each one. Isaac was delighted. He'd never shown the tin to anyone. A treasure tin was secret and there was no point in showing people secret things because they stopped being secret, but the girl had seen it already so it didn't matter. He thought she wouldn't be interested but she was. She listened attentively.

There were pictures of his mother and father, carefully painted faces in small, oval frames. There were two lenses, one concave, one convex.

"I got these from a teacher," he said proudly.

"What for?" Lisi asked.

"To see things clearly," said Isaac. "But they are not very good. I would like to make something that can look much closer at everything."

"Like the stars?" said Lisi.

"Yes. I have some ideas, but I need to plan it out better. I'm not clever enough yet."

Lisi thought him clever enough to get through any tests that she'd ever taken, just for fun. He would probably make mincemeat of the national curriculum.

"What's this?" she asked.

She held a small, circular metal container.

"Press the button at the top," said Isaac.

She pressed it and the lid popped open. Inside were about ten old coins. Lisi tipped them into her hand.

"Use the lens," said Isaac.

Lisi used the concave one and the coins appeared even smaller. Isaac laughed, but in a nice way, and gave her the other lens. Lisi studied the first coin.

"It's Roman," said Isaac. "A denarius. It's made of silver."

To Lisi it looked like a battered bottle top, but Isaac was fascinated by it and by the other coins. He told her what they were made of and when they were made.

And that was when the penny dropped.

She stared at the coins, then at Isaac.

"What year is this?" she asked.

Isaac thought she meant the coin.

"About 50 AD, the time of ...."

"No, this year, now."

Isaac thought Lisi was joking.

"You know which year it is," he said. "Why should you ask me?"

"Just tell me!" said Lisi.

Isaac sighed, took a deep breath as if about to explain the most simple thing to a child and said, "This is the year of our Lord 1652. Which year did you think it was?"

Lisi went white. She should have guessed, but it was too unreal to guess. She sat down on Isaac's bed in case she fainted.

"What's wrong?" Isaac asked. "Are you ill?"

"Maybe," said Lisi. "I must be dreaming after all."

"I don't think so," said Isaac. "We can't both be dreaming. And I'm real enough. Have you discovered something. I like disc..."

"This is the past," she whispered. "And I am in your future."

Isaac stood stock still. He turned her words over in his peculiar mind where they sounded more peculiar than ever.

"Don't be absurd."

"I am not being 'absurd'," said Lisi. "Through there," she pointed to the wooden panelling, "it's the year 2016."

Isaac stared into at the wall as if it was challenging him to make sense of Lisi's idea.

"Nonsense," he said.

"Yes, it is, isn't it," said Lisi. "But it has to be true. I'm from hundreds of years into the future."

"Three hundred and sixty-four," said Isaac whose mental arithmetic was second to none.

"Something like that," she said.

"No, exactly like that, if it's true, which it can't be."

"Wait!" she said, and without warning she dashed through the arch. Isaac stared after her, inspected the wooden panel and began to panic again. Perhaps he was going mad. He'd always feared it. He was too clever for his own good and cleverness could turn your wits inside out. He held his breath, wondering if the girl had gone for good, even if she had ever been there at all.

A minute later she returned.

"Look!" she said.

She held a coin in her hand and gave it to Isaac. He weighed it in his own hand and studied it carefully. The date was '2008'.

"Where did you get this?" he asked.

"From my purse," said Lisi. "I couldn't find one that said this year. I mean my 'this year'. Now do you believe me?"

Isaac rubbed the coin and even bit it, tasting the metal. He used the lens to look at the image of Queen Elizabeth and read the Latin words as easily as any alphabet.

"I've always thought time linear," he muttered.

"What?" said Lisi.

"I've always thought time ran in a straight line."

"Doesn't it?" she asked.

Isaac shook his brilliant head and said in a most wise and adult way, "I need to give this considerable thought."

Lisi stood up and said firmly, "I'm going back, Isaac, for good. I'm scared."

Isaac touched her gently on the shoulder.

"Please don't go! There's so much to talk about!"

"Yes, there is, isn't there?" Lisi replied, "but I want to go back now. You have to understand."

A cloud of anger hung over Isaac and his eyes darkened.

"No, I don't understand! No one ever does what I want! I might as well be invisible."

"You're not invisible. I can see you!"

"You know what I mean. I'm just in everyone's way. It's a hateful world!"

Lisi was shocked at his outburst. All she was saying was that she had to go home, back to her time.

"I'm tired," she said.

"I'm not!" hissed Isaac. "Why don't you stay and talk to me? There's so much to say. I want to learn about your home. You can't go, not now!"

Lisi was adamant.

"I can go and I am going. You shouldn't make such a fuss. Laura and Adam will be worried if they see my bedroom empty."

"Who?"

"My foster parents. Effdee and Effem. I told you. Look, I'll come back. I promise. We can talk. And maybe I'll bring Laszlo with me. You'll like him."

Actually, Lisi wasn't sure that Isaac would like him or that Laszlo would like Isaac, but she didn't want to return alone. Isaac would have none of it.

"No you won't come back! I don't believe you!"

"I will, if I can, that's a promise."

Isaac hesitated, then said, "Don't spy on me first! I don't want you spying on me."

"Alright," Lisi agreed. "Now shake hands."

"No."

Lisi shrugged. She didn't know whether to feel anger or sympathy for Isaac. Was he spoiled or was he neglected, she wasn't sure. But he was certainly demanding. She waved as she headed for the wooden panel. He didn't wave back. He looked furious, then he started crying. Lisi sighed, went over and gave him a quick hug, then vanished.

She'd promised not to spy on him so she tried not to peek when she was back in her bedroom, but she hardly had a chance. The light in the arch was fading and the very last thing she saw was Isaac fumbling along the wooden panel in his room, trying to see if he could figure out where his mysterious night visitor had gone and whether there was a way he might reach in to bring her back.

7. Laszlo

"What was his name?"

"Isaac," said Lisi.

Laszlo sat opposite her in the school library. She had spoken to him more in the past few days than she had in the past few months, ever since she arrived, silent and serious. He'd liked her straight away, maybe because he could also be silent, even if it was for different reasons, but she kept herself to herself. Until now, she had no real friends at all, but here she was talking to him.

And what was she saying, Laszlo asked himself? Nonsense!

He was starting to believe that Lisi wasn't just quiet but that she wasn't quite all there either, only he was too nice to back away and leave her totally friendless. If she really needed someone to tell these tall stories to, well, he'd listen, there was no harm in that.

"So the arch woke you up?"

"Yes."

"And you saw this Isaac on the other side?"

"Yes."

"And you went through into his room?"

"Yes."

"And he was angry?"

"Not at me, at everything. I think... I think he liked me, but he's not used to being friendly."

"Why not?"

Lisi looked down and said, "People have their reasons."

Laszlo didn't want to catch Lisi out, he wanted her to feel that he was taking her seriously, even though it was obvious that she was making the whole thing up.

"And he was clever?" he asked.

"Yes, like you."

Now that made Laszlo blush. He wasn't normally the blushing type but he went a touch red. He'd always felt he understood things quickly and wanted to know more than he already knew. This might have been because he never felt totally English. His mum and dad had come to England from Poland just before he was born, so he was well and truly English, but why oh why had they named him Laszlo? It seemed silly to him that they came to live in England then pretended they were still Polish! It made him feel different and out of place, but his parents said that being different was good, it would strengthen him. He trusted his mum and dad and he always tried to do his best, but when he grew up he would probably change his name to Les or Larry or something like that.

"Okay. But what year did he say it was, this clever clogs?"

"Sixteen fifty two."

"Like three hundred and something years ago?"

"Three hundred and sixty-four. He worked it out straight away, without thinking."

That immediately made Laszlo even more doubtful. No one could work out big numbers like that without thinking. This story was definitely fake, but he didn't tell Lisi that she was making it up. He felt sorry for her.

Whatever was going on in her head wasn't her fault and she needed someone to talk to, so he would be the one. Everyone else in school might think she was too broody and miserable but he liked her company so he went along with the tall tale.

"Right," he said, "like Doctor Who."

"Doctor Who is television," said Lisi. "This happened."

"I know, but going back and forward in time, like he does?"

Lisi sat back and looked at the ceiling of the library. There were lights there that caught her eye and helped her focus. It had been five days since she'd popped through the arch to meet Isaac. Since then, the arch had remained quiet, no time tunnel antics, nothing at all. She was beginning to wonder if she'd really imagined it and if there was something wrong with her. She thought of telling Effem and Effdee but decided instead to tell Laszlo as he was a bit like Isaac, clever and quiet, but not so touchy, and he listened.

"You don't believe me, do you?" she asked, realizing how daft the story sounded.

"I don't know," said Laszlo, even though he did know. "You have to admit, it's strange."

"Yes, but it's true."

"But it hasn't happened again?"

"No."

"Why not?"

"I don't know why not! I wish I did!"

"Can I see it then?" he asked.

Laszlo had no idea what to expect and he wasn't sure what he would do once he'd convinced her that she'd been seeing things. He wanted her to trust him but it was an off-the-wall story. Lisi seemed to be deciding something, then she sighed, delved into her pink plastic handbag and carefully brought out something wrapped in white tissue paper.

"You can come and see it if you want," said Lisi, "but I brought part of it to show you."

She unwrapped the tissue paper revealing the spectacular glass heart of the cabinet. She'd been terribly unsure whether to bring it to school, but she knew that Laszlo would need proof. She watched as his eyes widened. He'd never seen anything so beautiful.

"Lisi!"

"I know, it's nice, isn't it?"

Laszlo picked it up. It was bigger than the span of his hand so he had to use two hands to hold it.

"Nice? It's fantastic! It must be worth millions!"

"Doesn't matter. I'm not going to sell it, am I? It comes from the cabinet."

Laszlo stared at the prism, turning it this way and that. Doubt entered his mind. He had been so sure that Lisi was making everything up, for whatever reason, but this beautiful glass ornament he held in his hands wasn't ordinary. It was special. He'd seen nothing like this, ever. It was warm and felt... well... powerful. How could it be? It was just glass or crystal but it made him nervous, as if it might do something unexpected, any moment.

"It isn't dangerous, is it?" he asked.

"I don't think so," said Lisi.

Laszlo held it up to the library window. Colours shot from the prism and hit the wall. They made him smile.

He looked into its heart but the more he looked, the deeper it drew him. There were reflections and refractions of the library, but there were other things too, only he couldn't make them out.

"It's the way you look at it," said Lisi.

Laszlo hardly heard her, he was so enthralled.

"How do you mean?" he said.

"I've spent ages staring into it," she said. "Sometimes I thought I could see Isaac again, but other times I thought I saw... well, things."

Laszlo knew that she was hiding something, and he guessed it was to do with her past. Everyone knew everything about everyone else's family in school, but no one knew anything about Lisi, except she was fostered. Her real past was a secret.

"You can tell me if you want," he said. "I won't tell anyone else."

She thought for a moment then said, "No, not now. Maybe another time. What can you see?"

He turned the prism a dozen different ways and saw a dozen different views of the library, but he was sure he also saw things that weren't in the library at all, things that couldn't be reflected in the crystal, unless it was the light playing tricks on him.

"Oh, this and that. Hard to make it out," he answered. "It's great Lisi, really great!"

"I thought I might take it to show Isaac next time I go. See what he thinks of it."

Laszlo put the prism down for a moment and said, as if the prism itself had made him want to ask, "Lisi, you're not making all this up, are you? I mean, this Isaac, is he really real? He's not like a made-up friend?

I don't mind if you tell me the truth," he said, as if the truth would embarrass her.

"I *am* telling you the truth. I met him. He's the most unhappy boy I've ever seen, and the cleverest too."

"Cleverer than me?"

"Maybe."

"I want to meet him," said Laszlo, not sure that he would like such a boy but also wanting to help Lisi get over this delusion of time travel.

He looked down at the prism resting on the table between them like a miniature pyramid. Even there it sent out tiny shards of colour and drew their attention. Laszlo smiled. He couldn't help smiling when he looked into it, but he didn't know why.

Although he was the same age as Lisi, he felt older. He felt older than all the children. He always had done, and this was because he'd had to grow up feeling different. Other boys had picked on him because of his name and at first he let them, but then he learned to fight back. He didn't like fighting and he couldn't understand it when he had to, but if he didn't then the bullies would keep on at him. They would make fun of his name and his country, even though they didn't know anything about it, and there were some things you just couldn't walk away from. But usually he was gentle and studious.

"I don't suppose you'd let me take it home?" he asked.

Lisi shook her head. She trusted him but the cabinet without the prism was just a hollow shell, a torch without a battery or a person without a heart.

"I can show you something else," she said, "if you're

interested."

"Course I am," said Laszlo, wondering what else could match the fascinating prism.

Lisi delved into her bag again and brought out the instruction manual.

Laszlo started to doubt himself. Could everything that Lisi had told him really be true? He thought of himself as a down-to-Earth sort of boy, clever but without much imagination, yet he doubted himself for a moment and wondered whether her adventure might truly have happened.

The manual was old and mysterious and when Lisi showed him how the centre pages worked, he raised his eyebrows.

"Cool," he said. "Fancy tablet. Better than anything I've ever seen."

It was better than the best computers either of them had ever seen. There was something special about it and Laszlo knew it.

"Did you make this yourself?" he said, studying the complicated drawings for the arch.

"Yes," said Lisi. "You have to be patient, that's all. You don't have to be clever."

Laszlo ran his finger over the instructions, watched them pop out and pop back, saw the scrolling lines, step by step numbers and immaculate diagrams.

"Clev...er!" he said.

He turned to the poem at the front and read what it said about models coming to life, then scratched his head.

"What wars, Lisi? Is it something to do with what happened to you, about your real mum and dad?"

She didn't answer and he didn't ask again. Her face had turned red, not with anger but with some deep and dreadful memories. Laszlo told himself to think more before he spoke. It was a bad habit and he had to break it. Lisi was too nice to upset, much too nice.

"Alright, suppose I believe you," said Laszlo. "What do you want me to do?" he asked.

"Come with me."

"But you said it only worked once."

"So far, but I think it will work again. I've always done everything by myself but I need to do this with a friend."

"Why?" asked Laszlo.

Lisi didn't have a good answer. She felt that the arch was waiting for her to make a choice, and this was it. Laszlo would go with her. The arch wasn't letting her through alone and the instruction had already told her to trust those who cared for her, and Laszlo seemed to care, even if he thought the story was made up.

Lisi didn't trust many people any more, not after all the things she'd seen, but Effem and Effdee were good people and so was Laszlo. He might balance things out a little if they got through the arch into Isaac's world. She wasn't sure how, but just by being a boy, Laszlo might make Isaac less suspicious. And he was suspicious. In a way, Lisi felt like she was looking in a mirror when she thought of him, all anger and doubt and loneliness.

"I wouldn't have brought the prism and book to school if I didn't want you to believe me and come with," said Lisi. "I thought of you. You can make it work again."

Laszlo screwed up his forehead. He was puzzled. If it was a joke, it was a complicated one, and if it wasn't a joke, what on Earth was it?

"Alright," he said. "but don't blame me if nothing happens. And it won't. I know it won't."

He didn't 'know' at all, not any more.

He didn't want to give the manual back to Lisi. It was such a wonderful book, almost alive in his hands, with moving words and pictures. It made the new computers everyone was talking about look stiff and awkward.

That night, at home, he researched 'prism'. There were all kinds of references, like comic characters and magazines and rock bands, but there was also a lot about light and colour. So what was so special about this one?

There were whole lots of complicated formula and, as clever as he was, Laszlo didn't understand them, but he was smart enough to see that prisms split light into all the colours of the rainbow. And light was refracted, or bent, and sometimes reflected like a mirror. They were fascinating things, used by scientists for hundreds of years.

Laszlo skipped down the names of these scientists but they meant nothing to him. Once, something twigged at the back of his mind, but it stayed at the back and didn't tell him why it was there. If it had, he might have had a brainwave, put two and two together and known that Lisi might actually be telling the truth, but it didn't tell him so he didn't tell her.

There were dozens of images telling him what a prism was and what it wasn't. No curves, he read. A cylinder could never be a prism, even if it was made of the clearest crystal. There were formulas that intrigued him, ones that could work out the length of its sides, the area of each end, how much it weighed and how much space it took up. There were regular and irregular prisms and calculations for working out how light found its way through them.

Many readers would have been lost in the letters and numbers and complicated names, but Laszlo was only slightly fazed. He sensed that in time, he could understand all this. At present, it was fascinating stuff, but all Key Stage One Hundred and Something in secondary school, or even university, not for a young swat like him and certainly not for a young swat three and a half centuries ago.

8. The King's School

"That's him!" whispered Lisi.

It was Saturday afternoon in Lisi's house. Laszlo had come round to see what there was to see, pretty sure, despite the prism and the book, that there would be nothing to see. But the arch had opened up almost as soon as he'd entered the room, a pale light shimmering and changing, filtering and forming. Into what, though?

They stared into the scene and it definitely wasn't a bedroom. It was a library, but not at all like the one they had at school. There wasn't a computer in sight, not even a paperback book. Every book was hard-bound in dark, weighty leather, older and grander than any they'd ever seen. Shelf upon shelf of these huge books loomed above a little boy who pored over one of them set upon a wooden desk, all alone in the daunting room.

"You were telling the truth!" Laszlo exclaimed, both astonished and apologetic. Lisi just looked at him as if to say that he should never have doubted her. "And that's him?" Laszlo asked. "Are you sure?"

Lisi was very sure. It was Isaac, and he was studying hard, his face a mixture of concentration and dark, brooding anger.

She popped the prism into her bag and said, "I told him I wouldn't snoop, so I won't. Let's go."

Without warning, she grabbed Laszlo's hand and pulled him into the archway. He didn't have time to pull back. He felt a peculiar tingling sensation, then Lisi's bedroom was gone and he was in the room he'd just been staring at through the arch.

Isaac might have heard something, but he certainly saw something. He turned sharply.

"You!" he said.

"Me," said Lisi. "I told you I'd come back."

"You told me that two years ago," said Isaac, a harsh, condemnatory tone in his voice.

"Two years! No it wasn't. It was last week!"

They stared at each other, wondering who was lying, but they were both telling the truth, only it made no sense.

"Who's that?" Isaac asked suspiciously, nodding towards Laszlo.

"I'm Laszlo," said Laszlo, staring around, trying to tell himself that this wasn't a dream, that he was part of some strange happening.

"I don't want you here," he heard the boy say.

That snapped him out of his reverie. Isaac was looking at him harshly.

"Doesn't matter what you want," said Laszlo without thinking. "I'm here. Lisi asked me to come and I'm her friend."

Isaac closed the book he'd been reading and faced his two visitors.

"It was only supposed to be you," he said to Lisi.

"No it wasn't," said Lisi. "I never said that. Besides, Laszlo's clever, like you, and he wanted to meet you."

Isaac found it hard to adjust. He had rarely received much more than abuse and punches from boys, and none of them had ever been able to talk his language, so he didn't see why this one should be any different.

"You should go back to where you came from," he said to Laszlo.

Laszlo replied, "You're not very friendly, are you?"

"I'm what I am," said Isaac.

They faced each other for a few moments then Isaac turned to Lisi and said, "You never came back. You lied to me."

"The arch didn't work," she said, "till just now. I think it only worked again because Laszlo came with me."

Isaac sniffed. He didn't like not understanding anything and there was too much here that he didn't understand at all.

"Where are we?" Lisi asked. "This isn't your home, is it?"

Isaac almost laughed, but he looked again at Laszlo and forced a frown.

"No. It's my new school. I've just started."

They were impressed by the school library, hardly believing a school would have books like this in a room like this. It was more like a museum or stately home.

Isaac had given up hope of seeing the strange girl again. Two years was a long, long time, and he'd decided that the whole thing had either been a dream or that his so-called friend Lisi was a liar, but she didn't look or sound like a liar now that she stood in front of him again.

"You do look older," she said to him.

"I *am* older," he said. "Two years older. I'm twelve, almost."

"This is definitely like Doctor Who," Laszlo

whispered to Lisi.

"What did you say?" said Isaac. "Don't whisper in front of me!"

"Nothing," said Laszlo. He was determined not to be intimidated by this strange, angry boy. "You wouldn't understand," he added, which was probably the worst thing he could have said.

"I understand more than you, more than anyone!" Isaac hissed.

"Good for you," said Laszlo.

Lisi came between them and said, "Isaac, Laszlo, don't argue, please. This is special. This is happening for a reason. Just try to get on. Isaac," she said gently, "I'm really sorry it's been two years for you. I don't see how it can be, but I believe you. It's only been a week for us."

Isaac's face changed, the anger seemed to subside, as if he had something new and very interesting to consider.

"Time is linear," he said, "it can't pass at different speeds for me and you."

"Well, I don't know what linear means," said Lisi, "but something has happened. You're a lot older but I'm still the same."

Isaac took a few moments to consider, then grudgingly admitted, "I suppose you might be telling the truth."

"Thanks," said Laszlo, with a touch of sarcasm. "I suppose you're telling the truth, too."

"Your name," said Isaac, "it isn't English. Where are you from?"

"Mars," said Laszlo. "Where are you from?"

"Why do you have such a foreign name?" asked Isaac, ignoring the question.

"Why are you so rude?" Laszlo asked in return.

Lisi had to intervene again.

"You two!" she said. "Will you try and be friends!"

"He insulted me," said Laszlo.

"I didn't. I just asked where you came from."

"And I just asked where you came from."

They glowered at each other, Isaac trying to work out why the mysterious girl had brought this idiot with her and Laszlo trying to see why his new best friend had brought him to see this bad tempered, stuck-up swat.

"Isaac," said Lisi. "Where are we?"

"You are in the library of The King's School, Grantham, Lincolnshire. Where did you think you were?"

"We didn't think anything," said Lisi, walking over to the window and looking out.

"Aren't you in the school too?" asked Isaac. He'd assumed they were both students there, just like him, only shifted out of time somehow.

Laszlo had joined Lisi and was staring at the magnificent buildings through the grand library window.

"Not likely," he said. "This is not like our school at all. It's not like any school I've ever seen, except on television. Is it any good?"

Isaac said it was the best in the country. He was enjoying his days at The King's School even if the boys, and even some of the masters, weren't as clever as him.

"I can show you around," he said quietly, making an effort at peace, "if you want."

"We'll be a bit... obvious, won't we?" said Lisi looking at their clothes.

"There's no one around," said Isaac. "It's holiday, but grandmother said I could stay, if I wanted, and I do. Of course I do. This is the best place on Earth."

Laszlo raised his eyebrows. 'The best place on Earth'? He could hardly imagine calling his own school that. But this was different, in every way, and Isaac was different too, very much so.

They followed him but he wasn't at ease and they had to keep asking him questions about where they were and what the buildings were for. Isaac gave brief, gruff answers and kept checking to make sure the two were still there and hadn't vanished.

The school was as impressive close up as it had been through the library window. Everything was built to last, especially the main hall which was frighteningly huge and made them feel even smaller than they were. Isaac did his best to lay aside his foul mood. He was proud of the school and wanted the visitors to like it, not just the bricks and mortar but what went on inside. Nevertheless, he was fidgety and seemed preoccupied. Halfway across the courtyard lawn he stopped and said, "Why have you come here? What do you want? Are you spies?"

"Spies!" Lisi and Laszlo exclaimed together.

"Why would we be spies?" asked Lisi.

Isaac shrugged. Knowledge was power and he'd been told that many countries were jealous of English schools so maybe these two children were spies for France or Spain.

"Haven't seen much to spy on," said Laszlo. "I mean,

it's big and grand and all that, but our school's got much more than this."

"How?" said Isaac. "That isn't possible! We have one of the best libraries in the country!"

"Okay, but books aren't everything, and yours are all old."

"Old!"

Lisi prodded Laszlo.

"He didn't mean that," she said, "they only look old. They would, wouldn't they Isaac, if what we've told you is true?"

Isaac stuck his hands in his pockets and brooded.

"What have you got that we haven't?" he asked.

"Equipment, for a start," said Laszlo.

"What equipment?"

"Just loads of science stuff. You know."

Isaac didn't know, but he dearly wanted to know. He especially wanted to know what they meant by the word 'science'.

"Tell me what... 'stuff'," he demanded.

Laszlo blew a deep breath and wondered how to describe his school to someone who had never heard of electricity, let alone televisions, smartphones, computers, wifi and a dozen other fancy gizmos. But he also had a sneaky feeling that despite the gizmos, there was something in Isaac and his old school that was much more valuable, only he didn't know quite what it was. He was saved from answering by a commanding voice.

"Ah, Mr..." said the commanding voice so scarily that neither Lisi nor Laszlo registered the name. "Who goes there with you?"

They saw a figure like Dracula walking towards them.

"Friends sir," said Isaac.

"I see," said the man who was tall and strict-looking. He stopped in front of them and peered at Lisi and Laszlo as if he was studying tiny creatures under a microscope. He appeared to realise they were human and said, "And they are?"

"Just visitors sir," answered Isaac.

"Hmm, strangely dressed visitors. You are from?"

"Foreign lands sir," said Isaac, "friends of my grandmother. They don't speak English."

The man towered over them, making them feel they were shrinking beneath his gaze, but he forced a smile and put a hand on Isaac's shoulder.

"And how is your grandmother, Isaac?"

"Well, sir."

"Good. And your mother?"

Isaac's face darkened. Lisi thought he was going to say something he'd be sorry for, but he held his tongue and just muttered, "Well too, sir."

"Glad to hear it. No more talk of taking you away from here?"

"No sir."

"Good. You're a fine student, Isaac."

"Thank you sir."

"Hmm. Your friends dress most strangely. Where did you say they were from, Isaac?"

"I didn't, sir."

"Quite, quite! So, I shall see you at the usual time for some extra Latin verse, Isaac?"

"Yes sir."

"Good. Hmm."

And he left, sweeping his cloak out as if attempting to fly away.

"He is my house master and Latin teacher," said Isaac. "As I'm here, he wants me to use my holiday time wisely, so he's giving me extra lessons."

Lisi and Laszlo stared after the disappearing teacher, waiting for him to turn into a bat or climb up the school walls, but he strode into the school buildings, leaving them a touch bewildered.

"He's a teacher?" Laszlo asked.

"Yes," said Isaac. "Why do you ask?"

"He looks... strict," said Lisi.

Isaac seemed surprised. Saying teachers were strict was like saying snow is white; they were never anything else.

They stopped again in the main hall where Isaac told them about the curriculum, which was mainly Latin and Greek, neither of which they'd heard of. This puzzled Isaac. Knowledge was power and these two children clearly had power of some kind, and yet they had no idea about anything that went on in this most respected school. What had happened to make them forget everything they'd been taught, unless they really hadn't been taught it at all?

Isaac showed them his sleeping quarters, a dormitory where, in term time, twenty or so other boys also slept. He sat down on his bed and his visitors sat on the one beside it. There was an awkward silence.

Laszlo was thinking of something the scary teacher had said. He hadn't called Isaac by his name but Mister Something Or Other – what was it? The name rang a bell but Laszlo couldn't remember why. The back of his mind was a store of unused information.

"What did he mean about your mother wanting to take you away?" asked Lisi.

Isaac kicked his legs back and forward in a restless way.

"She won't do it," he said. "If she does, I'll scream the house down. I won't go and live with *him*!"

"Who's 'him'?" Laszlo asked.

"My stepfather. I hate him and he hates me."

Lisi then did something quite unexpected, she leaned over and held Isaac's hand.

"You'll be alright," she said gently.

Isaac stared at her hand for a moment then pulled it away.

"I don't need sympathy," he said. "I just need him to disappear."

Lisi sat back and pretended to study the dormitory.

"I'm not surprised you get the miseries," she said. "This place is so dreary."

Isaac didn't think it was. This was normal, and he was unhappy for other reasons.

"I brought you something," said Lisi. "Here."

She opened her bag and took out the prism, wrapped in white tissue paper.

When Isaac saw it, his brooding mood vanished at once. He stood up, holding the prism in front of him as if it was the most precious thing in the universe.

"Where did you get it?" he asked. "It's... it's..."

"I told you," said Lisi, surprised by the effect the prism had on the unhappy boy. "It's the heart of the thing that lets us see you."

Isaac took the prism to the rather small dormitory window and studied it intently for a long while, then he suddenly turned to them and said, "I have so many ideas! Sometimes I think my head is going to explode. I think about so much and no one knows, not even the masters here. I thought they would, but they don't. They teach what they know, not learn what they don't know. I want to ask, but they aren't interested. And my stepfather is worst of all. He sees nothing but what is in front of him. I hate him. I can't go back to them. I have to stay here and learn, on my own, otherwise I will go mad."

Lisi and Laszlo listened to the passionate boy but weren't sure what to say, so they said nothing.

"I can't help it," Isaac went on, clutching the prism to his chest, "you probably think I'm mad already but I'm not." He gazed at the prism and said, "This is the best thing you could ever have brought me."

"But it's just glass," said Laszlo which almost brought out another fit of anger from Isaac, only he was in a rare good mood and his eyes flashed only for a fraction of a second.

"No it isn't. It's full of secrets," he said. "The biggest secrets in the universe. Can't you see that?"

Neither Lisi nor Laszlo were stupid, but they couldn't see it at all.

"I see God inside," said Isaac. Laszlo screwed up his nose and thought that the boy was not quite all there. "God as Truth!" said Isaac. "Not the God they tell us about but the way the world works! I see numbers and angles and geometries," he cried, holding the prism and looking into it as if he was looking into himself. "Most of all I see light, and light is at the heart of the universe. I want to know what it is, how fast it travels, what it's made of, where it comes from, where it goes, I want to know everything about it! You," he said to the two wary listeners, "don't you also want to know these things?"

Lisi and Laszlo exchanged looks. They were feeling rather sheepish. This boy was three hundred and fifty years behind them in time but about a thousand years ahead of them in understanding. They both felt quite ignorant next to Isaac who evidently saw things in a different way to them and knew, or wanted to know, more than they would probably ever know.

"We do learn," said Laszlo. "It's just... well... a bit different at school."

"I don't mean school!" Isaac said. "Here, I learn Greek and Latin and a little arithmetic but *here*," he pointed to his head, "this is my real school! And this!" He pointed to the prism. "It means something to me. As soon as I saw it, I knew!"

"Knew what, Isaac?" Lisi asked quietly.

"That there is so much to find out," said Isaac, "and that the answers are really there, if you know how to look for them. Can I keep this?"

Lisi gently took the prism back from Isaac.

"If I gave it to you," she said, "we wouldn't be able to get home again. It's part of the cabinet, part of the kit, the most important part."

"Cabinet! Kit!" cried Isaac. "Let me see it! Let me come with you. I don't want to lose this," he said, pointing to the prism.

Lisi could think of a thousand reasons why Isaac shouldn't come with her, the main one being that he simply couldn't. He'd tried, last time, and hit the wood panel. This was his time and he couldn't get out of it...

Unless...

Lisi grabbed his hand and said, "Alright, let's try!"

"Hey Lisi!" said Laszlo. "What are you doing?"

"Let's get back to the library," shouted Lisi. "Quick!"

Isaac was flabbergasted. He'd never been pulled around like this, but for some reason he trusted the girl. Besides, she had the prism and he didn't want to lose sight of it.

They reached the library and with great relief saw Lisi's bedroom beyond the misty arch.

"Hold on to my hand Isaac," said Lisi. "What can you see?"

Isaac gripped her hand and stared into what seemed like a vision of colour and unreal things, things to which he could give no name.

"I... I..."

"Good!" said Lisi, knowing that Isaac could see her room if he held on to her. "Laszlo, you go first."

Laszlo walked into the arch and they saw him trickle away into the distance.

"Now Isaac, follow me and don't let go."

So saying, she walked through the archway, pulling the flustered boy with her.

In the twinkling of an eye, Isaac had left the safety of his ancient school and set foot into the twenty-first century.

9. The Science Museum

"Well, what do you think?"

Lisi let go of Isaac's hand and watched as the astonished boy gaped at the new world in Lisi's bedroom.

"Where is this?" he asked in a terrified whisper.

"My bedroom," said Lisi. "In the year 2016. I told you. That's the arch, that's the cabinet and it's all true."

Isaac looked around, amazement etched into his face at every new thing that he saw. Through the archway he could still see the library, shimmering as if part of a vision.

"Is this magic?" he asked.

"I don't know what it is," said Lisi. "You're the clever one, you tell me."

Very carefully, she put the prism back in the centre of the cabinet and as she did so, the arch faded and The King's School with it.

"My home!" said Isaac.

Lisi took the prism back and the King's School reappeared.

"It will let you back when you want," said Lisi. "Do you want to go now?"

Isaac hesitated. He was scared, but he was still alive and breathing and every instinct told him to wait and see, to see and to learn. He couldn't run away home like a scared baby. He shook his head.

Lisi put the prism back, The King's School faded again but Isaac remained, startled and anxious. He felt a hand on his shoulder. It was Laszlo.

"You alright?" Laszlo asked. "You look a bit pale."

Isaac pushed Laszlo's hand away and wandered around the bedroom, not speaking, touching everything, checking everything, his dark eyes focused like lasers. They let him explore, hardly daring to speak. They might not have said anything at all for a long while but there was a knock on the door and they froze. Isaac turned as if the devil had rapped on his head.

Effem opened the door and peeked in.

"Everything alright Li... oh, hello!" she said, seeing two strange boys skulking around, one in fancy dress. Laszlo said hello and introduced himself but Isaac didn't answer and stared at Laura with frightened eyes.

"This is Isaac," said Lisi. "He's a new boy. Laszlo and I just met him. He's a bit shy."

Effem held out her hand. Isaac stared at it but didn't make a move to shake it. Effem guessed this was because of nerves rather than rudeness and said, "Adam and I are thinking of going out. Would you like to come?"

Lisi was tempted to say no as Isaac had only just stepped foot into her world, but then she thought that her bedroom was not a particularly exciting place so going out would be good.

"Yes, thank you."

Something was different about Lisi but Laura wasn't sure what – her eyes sparkled more and she seemed a little more confident and happier, but perhaps that was only wishful thinking.

"We thought of visiting The Science Museum. Haven't been there for a while and Adam's keen to see the Children's Gallery for some reason. He just won't grow up, will he. Interested?"

Lisi wondered how and why things sometimes happened the way they did. Was it an invisible god pulling invisible strings? The Science Museum! Perfect. She glanced at Isaac but didn't mention that he was a swat who talked about light and God and geometry and that a visit to The Science Museum was the best possible choice, she just said they'd be ready in two minutes. Any longer and he might change his mind.

Isaac didn't say a word. It was as if he'd been struck dumb. He did everything that was asked, including a minor change of jacket to look slightly more modern, even if the jacket was Lisi's. Isaac stared at himself in the mirror as if he was looking at a stranger.

If Lisi's bedroom had startled him, the rest of the house, the street and finally the car bewildered him totally. He said nothing at all, but seemed to take in every detail and be making giant leaps in his brain which was working overtime. His eyes, normally dark and often screwed up in anger were opened wide in continual astonishment. There was nothing, absolutely nothing, of his own world, not a speck of dust that told him he was on the same planet as the one he'd left just minutes earlier. Instead, he was in a wonderland of inexplicable devices and unimaginable works. Every street was lined with a mind-boggling array of marvels and he was travelling along them in something that powered itself, without horses pulling it along.

In the sky he saw arrow-straight trails of white and

silver which Lisi told him were aeroplanes carrying people across the globe. He heard but he couldn't understand. How was this possible? There was nothing in his own vision of the world that suggested people could travel without horses pulling them or fly across the sky in tubes of metal.

And there were lights. Even during the day he could see that the city was powered by something wonderfully bright. There were lights inside and outside so that no corner remained dark. He wondered if the light stayed on at night and what the city must look like then. He wondered but he didn't ask. He couldn't speak. His voice was trapped inside as he struggled to see and hear all there was to see and hear.

And he heard so much, he almost had to cover his ears. Never had he heard such noises. Even at school where a hundred students might talk together, there was nothing like this. This was a stupendous riot of noise, not just voices but sounds from a thousand mysterious places. It was as if every quiet space in his head was filled with some noise or other. He felt giddy with it. How could anyone think with this endless, unceasing sound? Even in the car, as they called it, with the windows down he could hear mysterious noises and, when the window was opened, the sounds of the city rolled in like a tidal wave of chaos.

They drove to a station on the underground at which point Isaac almost ran for his life. It wasn't just the surface of the Earth that was full of people, but inside it too! People flocked down moving stairs into the bowels of the Earth, and climbed aboard monstrous engines that pounded along with thunderous noise and bone-rattling shakes.

He held Lisi's arm with a grip of iron and she had to ask him to loosen up, but he was afraid of what might happen if he let her go, that he might slip off the monster and fall, all alone. He had never felt so helpless and vulnerable in all his few years of life.

People looked at him and he stared back, trying to make out whether they were real and whether this whole thing was a nightmare. He studied every detail of the train and stared at the electric lights as if they held the secret of everything, like the prism. He rubbed his eyes when the light made them sore, then stared again, sure that he would be able to see what made them burn so brightly.

At the stations, he thought he was being taken to Hades and back, the darkness of the Earth about to swallow him up. The inside of the world had been carved out and shaped so that people could wander around, in and out, up and down as if it was the most normal thing. And it was lit again, as the shops had been, so that there was no darkness, none at all! What should have been black was shining bright as if lit by a million candles, yet there was not a single candle in sight.

How long they travelled he had no idea, but he knew from the speed of the car and the train that they had travelled a long way, miles and miles, a distance that a carriage would take days or weeks to cover.

When he emerged into the light he beheld a world that was too vast to register. Buildings towered on every side and there were more people around than he thought existed on the whole of Earth. A sea of people crushed him so that he could barely stand.

"Hold on Isaac," said Lisi. "You're doing fine."

He held her again as they weaved in and out of the crowds to the entrance of a great marble building which Lisi told him was The Science Museum and which he might find interesting. He didn't know what a museum was, but he soon found out.

Something changed when he entered the museum. He felt the solidity of the building and a kind of peacefulness, despite the crowds. Most importantly, he felt safer, far safer than in the streets beyond the museum doors. He let go Lisi's hands and wandered away.

"Isaac!" Lisi called after him, but he didn't even turn. He probably didn't hear her, or if he did, he took no notice. "Isaac! Wait!"

He didn't wait. He had a feeling that he was in his element, like a fish in water, and set off on his own exploration of the museum.

"Funny boy," said Effem. "Is he... you know... alright, Lisi?"

"He's fine," said Lisi. "Laszlo, let's follow him, make sure he doesn't do any damage."

They made arrangements with Effem and Effdee to meet in an hour and set off in pursuit of Isaac. This wasn't difficult as he was walking slowly, looking at everything in close detail, trying to read as much as he could and press buttons wherever there were buttons to press.

Lisi and Laszlo did their best to explain things, but he didn't say a word in return. He was oblivious to them and to anyone else. All he could see were the exhibits, thousands of them, far too many to take in on a single visit. They couldn't even direct him. He found his own way everywhere, unable to take his eyes off the great steam engines dominating the ground floor.

Eventually he found the staircase to the children's gallery and once again studied every exhibit with his big, dark eyes, seeing what other children were doing and trying the same thing himself. Lisi and Laszlo followed him like shadows, thinking that they could explain things to him, but he didn't listen. He read and watched and made as much sense of it all as a three hundred year old mind that had never heard of electricity, let alone steam, could manage. He asked them nothing at all and never answered a single question. He didn't acknowledge them, or nod in answer to their questions. They might have thought him rude, but he wasn't being rude at all, he was in his own space, doing his own private learning.

He would wait far longer at one exhibit than anyone else. If they'd let him, he might have spent ages at just one stand, but they had at least to try and move him on. When time was up, he was nowhere near ready to meet up with Lisi's foster parents, so Laszlo stayed with him whilst Lisi went back and they arranged to meet in another hour.

They had managed to cover every floor, which had meant rushing him through some exhibits, something Isaac resented. He seemed to find it hard to leave anything that he hadn't studied intently. He had seen nameless wonders that burned brightly in his mind, machines that travelled through earth, air, fire and water; he had even seen machines that travelled beyond the Earth into space. He had seen examples of power far beyond anything he or his schoolmasters could ever comprehend and he didn't want to leave them, not for a moment. He had never felt at home as much as he felt there, by every exhibit on every floor. He had never been happier. How much he understood of it all was questionable, but he never tired of looking. Behind him, Lisi and Laszlo followed like servants, making sure he was alright and worrying that he might do something stupid, but he never did. They grew tired but he grew stronger. All they could think about was getting a drink and something to eat, but food and drink never entered their strange visitor's mind.

They had managed, at last, to get him into the cafeteria where he studied the tray of fizzy drink and sandwiches as if it was another exhibit. He drank and ate, inspecting the brown fizzy liquid and soft bread after each mouthful, as if it might poison him. Without warning, he left them, hurrying back to the optics department where he gazed at prism after prism, experiment after experiment. In the subdued lighting where the optics displays glowed brightly and beautifully, he was at one with the world. Lisi and Laszlo kept their eye on him, wondering what was going on his busy little head.

Something still played on Laszlo's mind, but he couldn't sort it out. He knew he had two and two somewhere in his memory, but couldn't make four. It was to do with the research he had done and something he had heard, but he couldn't figure out what was missing or what it meant.

More time was allowed and then a little more until the museum was about to close. This made no difference to Isaac. He looked as though he had become one of the exhibits and would rather have died than leave the building. It was a massive effort to get him to the door at closing time. He was distracted at every turn by something he thought he'd missed, but they had to be firm. At one point he grew angry and his eyes flared, but then something would occur to him and he calmed down.

"Did you enjoy it, Isaac?" asked Effdee.

Isaac didn't answer. He still hadn't spoken a word.

"I used to come here with my father," said Effdee, "especially the children's gallery. Fascinating."

As they left, Isaac gripped Lisi's hand again, looking back one last time into the magical space beyond.

"We have to go," said Lisi. "They close now, Isaac. Honestly. We have to go home."

The journey back was as silent as the journey there, at least for Isaac. He remained in a world of his own, not responding to any questions, making Effem and Effdee wonder about him, but they felt more sorry for him than anxious, thinking that he might need some special educational support at school. If they'd had any clue of the whirring and clunking in his brilliant mind, they would have been amazed, but he kept all his thoughts to himself.

Just before they arrived back, Adam asked Isaac whether he wanted them to take him home. He looked at them, puzzled.

"Don't worry," said Lisi. "We'll take him back later. He's got some stuff to collect from my room first."

Isaac was staring out of the car window with an unreadable expression. Adam didn't know what was going on, but something was definitely happening but he knew better than to push Lisi with questions. He trusted her and was sure she would never do anything wrong.

The arch was quiet when they entered Lisi's bedroom. Laszlo touched it but nothing happened.

"What if he's stuck here forever?" he asked.

Lisi shook her head.

"That won't happen," she said.

Isaac stood in front of the cabinet and examined it, opening the drawers, checking the pieces that were left and had not been used in the making of the arch, then took out the instruction manual. He sat down on Lisi's bed with the book on his lap and ran his finger down the opening page, reading as best he could what was to him a very different kind of English. As with Lisi and as with Laszlo, new words appeared. Isaac almost threw the book down in shock, but he held on as Lisi and Laszlo peered over his shoulder.

You who have seen what you have seen,
But doubt so much where you have been.
You whose anger pure as snow,
Clouds now what you think you know.

You whose mind and troubled heart
Baffled is by such great Art,
Be wise and clear as is the sky,
You can see clearly if you try.

You whose soul so restlessly
Searches for eternity,

Be you sure and calm and still,
In time you'll understand, you will.

All mysteries shall fade and die,
Till then, be true. Now bid goodbye.

Isaac ran his fingers up and down, watching the lettering rise and fall, seeing if he could tell how it vanished into the page. Finally, he put the book back into the top drawer of the cabinet.

"I must return home," he said, which were the first and only words he'd said since Lisi had brought him into the twenty-first century.

"Did you have a good day?" she asked.

Isaac thought about this for a few moments, then said, "I have much to think about."

"Don't think too hard," said Laszlo, "it isn't good for you."

Isaac did something he thought he could never do when he'd first met Laszlo what seemed like a lifetime before, he smiled at him.

"Look!" said Lisi.

They turned to see the archway shimmering and changing again. Through it they could see the great hall of The King's School. It was empty.

"Holidays still," said Isaac. "Will we meet again?"

"We'll try," said Lisi. "Bye."

Without a wave or any other sign, Isaac turned and strode through the arch.

Lisi and Laszlo could still see him in the great hall, but they weren't sure if he could see them. He turned to stare, but it seemed as if he was searching for something that wasn't there. He turned away, walked to a door at the far end of the library, opened it, stood still for a moment and turned back. He peered, slightly to the left, slightly to the right, as if searching them out, then nodded, as if acknowledging something or perhaps thanking them, knowing they were looking, strode out and closed the door behind him.

"Weird boy," said Laszlo.

"Weird day," said Lisi as the arch light flecked, fizzled and faded.

10. Family Matters

Over the next few days, Lisi waited for the arch to reignite, but it never did. Laszlo came round and they checked all the bricks to make sure none had fallen out, but it made no difference, the arch remained silent and still. Lisi was tempted to dismantle the whole thing, but it had taken her so long to build and looked so grand that she didn't have the heart to take it to pieces. Besides, she felt that the cabinet had something more to do and she had to stick with it.

They both wanted to see Isaac again, particularly Lisi. Laszlo was a little jealous although he secretly quite liked the bad tempered boy who had visited their century without uttering a word. They thought that in some small way they were helping him, and that in his small way he was helping them.

"I feel sorry for him," said Lisi as she lay in her favourite place in the garden staring up at the sky. Laszlo lay with his feet facing her feet, also staring towards a rich blue heaven.

"Lots of children's parents split up," said Laszlo. "It isn't the end of the world."

"It might feel like it," said Lisi, "and things were different then."

"How?"

"I don't know exactly, but he was just dumped. No one cared. At least there are people now who want to help."

"Lisi?" Laszlo asked, quietly. She didn't answer but she knew what was coming. "What happened to your mum and dad?"

She didn't answer. Of the few people she knew, Laszlo was now the one she would talk to if she talked at all, but she couldn't tell him what had happened. The words just wouldn't sound right, and most important, she wasn't sure. She knew what she'd been part of, a war in a far off country. People here had seen it on television, which meant that they could turn it off whenever they felt like it, but she couldn't do that. It had been with her then and it was still with her now. Real war was like that, you couldn't switch it off; it hurt you forever.

"Lost," she said. "I don't know if they're alive or not. I wish I did but I don't."

"But you have Effem and Effdee? And he has his grandmother."

"His mother left him to marry someone. She could have taken him with her."

"Maybe they didn't have enough money."

"Maybe they didn't have enough love."

"He makes a big fuss about it."

"Laszlo! He can't help it! He's been abandoned! That's the worst thing that can happen to anyone."

"What, worse than what happened to you?"

Lisi thought it was. What happened to her and to many others was awful, but it wasn't choice. Her mum didn't pack her bags and say, "I'm off sweetie-pie, have a nice life," and head out into the sunset with another dad. She'd been taken away, like her father had been taken away. They still loved her, if they were alive. Isaac's mum had disowned him. No wonder he was furious with everyone.

"I wonder what he's doing now," she said. "Do you think he remembers what happened?"

"He probably thinks he dreamed it all."

"Did we? I mean, it's far out, isn't it?"

Laszlo had been over what happened a hundred times, from the moment he'd spoken to Lisi in the school library through the visit to The King's School and then to The Science Museum. Time had been turned inside out, which wasn't possible, and yet it had happened! He still had the nagging feeling that he was missing something, a clue of some kind, and that irritated him, but he couldn't discover it.

He'd considered telling his family, a very large one of three brothers and three sisters, not to mention his mum, dad and countless aunts, uncles and cousins, but he decided against that – they would probably take him to a doctor or tell him off for lying. He was the odd one out in his family, very studious and quiet, maybe because he was smack in the middle, but he didn't mind that. He was comfortable with who he was and now he had a good friend in Lisi. He liked her a lot. She was clever and thoughtful and had secrets which made her special. He felt sorry for her because of all that had happened, even though she didn't want him, or anyone, feeling sorry for her.

"It's all good, though," said Laszlo, wrapping some grass around his fingers to help him concentrate.

"Is it?" Lisi asked.

"Yes," said Laszlo wisely, "because nothing clever

enough to help you build that arch would let bad things happen."

"It can't bring his mother back," said Lisi. "It can't make him happy. I'm worried about him."

"You don't know what it can or can't do," said Laszlo. "And you shouldn't worry about him, he'll be alright. He looked happy enough when he left."

"We have to find out," said Lisi. "I can't sleep not knowing if he's okay. He's all alone. We have to get back to him, Laszlo. I've sat up every night waiting for the arch to come to life but it just sits there doing nothing."

"You have to be patient," said Laszlo. "It's obviously not ready yet."

"Maybe it will never be ready, or maybe it's done whatever it had to do. I should take it to bits and build something else."

"Build what?" Laszlo asked. "You have to do what the instruction book tells you and it hasn't told you anything more, has it?"

It hadn't. She'd run her fingers up and down the pages but nothing had happened. It seemed to have said everything it wanted to say. She knew the verses off by heart and thought about them every day. One of them popped into her head now:

I'll give you hope where you have none,
And let you see what can be done.

Did she have hope? After all she'd seen and all she knew that people could do to each other, was she more hopeful than before? It was so hard to know. She felt the same, but Effem and Effdee said she looked happier. She didn't mean to be happy, not on purpose, because it was impossible to be happy in a world where terrible things happened, wasn't it? And who had she met that had 'left their mark'? Just one furious little boy, and if he'd left his mark, she didn't know what or where it was. How puzzling!

At supper that evening, Effem and Effdee were happier than Lisi could remember. They'd begun to feel that Lisi was at last accepting them as her foster parents. They never wanted to replace her birth parents but they wanted her to be content. The jackpot prize had something to do with it although they had no idea how or why. They asked her if she was going to take the arch down and build something new - after all, it had been up a while now.

"I've talked about it with Laszlo," said Lisi, "but we think we should leave it until... erm..."

"Until what, Lisi?"

"Until we know what to make next," she said, not wanting to tell them that the boy they'd met had popped out of the arch from a long gone century and that she and Laszlo were hoping to pop back into his life once again. The last thing she wanted was for Effdee and Effem to think she was lying. She didn't like keeping this secret from them but she didn't have a choice. They were good foster parents but they would never believe such a story and would start worrying about her.

"Since you won that prize," said Effem, "you've changed so much Lisi."

"Have I?"

"We think so," said Effdee.

"I'm trying to see things differently," said Lisi..

"That's not easy," said Effem.

"No," said Lisi, "but Isaac..."

"Isaac? That boy…"

"Yes. He's special. I... I feel sorry for him."

"Why? I thought you hardly knew him."

"I know him enough. I know how sad he is inside. I feel close to him. He's made me see what happened to me in a different way."

"Well, invite him to tea. Let's be kind to him. He sounds as though he needs some TLC."

Lisi couldn't think of any excuses so she said she would. She hoped her cheeks weren't too red.

More days passed and the arch remained stubbornly quiet. Lisi studied the instruction book every night and tried her best to get new lines to appear, but the book was just a book and didn't do anything spectacular or give her any idea of what it had in mind. She began to believe again that it had done all it had to do, that she really might as well take the arch down and either build something new or give up completely and treat the cabinet as a fancy chest of drawers, but her heart told her otherwise, that she had to be patient, that there was still more magic, if magic it was. This might have been wishful thinking but she simply couldn't dismantle the arch. It was still so wonderful to look at even if it didn't open up to any peculiar places. She never forgot to look and never gave up hope, just accepting it was there, waiting, sleeping.

It was the night of her thirteenth birthday as she lay on her bed reading that, for no apparent reason, it sprang into life. Her birthday had been a muted affair, a mixture of celebration and troubled memories. She'd felt the importance of it. Thirteen! It was a big and important number and the arch seemed to know it. There it was again, flowing with colours, dazzling, so beautiful to look at, shimmering up and down, down and up, alive with energy, calling to her. She waited a moment, pinched herself, saw what she saw and thought at a hundred miles an hour. Should she call Laszlo and tell him? No, there wasn't time. She had to act. This was the moment and if she had to go alone, there was a reason for it. She had faith in the wonderful vision joining her little bedroom to another place, another time.

She leaped out of bed, dressed hurriedly and, full of expectation, headed yet again into the unknown.

11. Fury

Three boys were swinging punches at Isaac who was swinging punches back again with a face of fury. He was older than he ought to have been, probably about fourteen or fifteen. Lisi blinked to make sure it was him, but it was, no doubt.

Without thinking, Lisi dived in and smacked into the back of one of the attackers, knocking him to the ground. He looked up in surprise and said, "Good Lord, Humphrey, it's a girl!"

The fight stopped and the other two attackers stared at the mad girl who had appeared out of nowhere. You simply didn't hit girls, not if you were a good public school boy, which is what the three attackers were supposed to be, so they didn't know what to do when she turned and walloped another one of them on the nose.

"How dare you!" she screamed. "He's one and you're three! You cowards!"

The boy who had been knocked down got up and brushed himself down.

"You're a girl, drat it! Girls are not supposed to fight!"

Lisi squared up to him and said, "And you're a boy. You're supposed to play fair."

Isaac was staring at her as if she was a ghost come to haunt him, but the fight was over, he knew it. The three boys pushed both Isaac and Lisi away, nonchalantly tidying themselves up and smoothing their hair.

"He started it," said Humphrey. "He landed the first punch."

"And I'll land the last," said Isaac, getting ready to start again, but Lisi moved closer to stop him.

"Fight's over," she said. "Go home."

"Come on chaps," said Humphrey. "Izzy's brought reinforcements. Saved you this time, Izzy."

"I don't need anyone to save me," said Isaac. "I'd knock you all down for sixpence."

He was so angry, Lisi wondered what they'd said or done to make him throw the first punch, but she believed him. He looked mad enough to take on thirty bullies, let alone three.

They tidied themselves up but still hung around, waiting to see what would happen, and maybe find out who she was.

"Well?" Lisi said to all three of them. "What are you waiting for? An invitation to get lost?"

"Who are you?" Humphrey asked.

"None of your business," said Lisi. "And if you're still here in ten seconds I'm calling the police."

"The what?" asked Humphrey.

None of them appeared to have any idea what she meant.

"I wouldn't hang around to see," Lisi said. "Why don't you all clear off, thugs."

They laughed, but it was nervous laughter. They were afraid of her, an unknown quantity and called it a day. There was no way they were going to swap fisticuffs with a girl, particularly as they might well lose.

Reputations could be tarnished forever in such a scrap.

"Takes a girl to save you then," said Humphrey.

Once again, Isaac was going to push past Lisi and lay into Humphrey but Lisi put a hand on his shoulder.

"No point," she said. "They're all thick as bricks. You couldn't knock any sense into them."

The three bullies gave Isaac threatening looks and made dismissive gestures to Lisi, but they wandered off all the same, faking laughter. Lisi and Isaac watched them until they turned a corner and disappeared.

"I would have beaten them," said Isaac then looked at Lisi, studying her face, remembering as if it were yesterday. "It's two years," he said. "I thought you'd never come back."

"Really? Two years? It's only been a few weeks for me," she said.

There was a small garden close by and Isaac took Lisi there, casting furtive glances at her to make sure she was all present and correct. It was distubing having a friend who popped in and out of his life so rarely and unexpectedly.

"You've got blood on your lip," said Lisi. "And on your nose. Here."

She started to dab his lip and nose with a handkerchief, but he took it from her, albeit politely and gently, and did it himself. He was quite a bit taller than she remembered, certainly taller than her now. She'd been taller than him last time they'd met.

"Thank you. I never thought to see you again."

"Well, here I am. The arch wouldn't open till now."

"Where is the boy?"

"Laszlo? He's okay. He wasn't around when it

happened."

Isaac sat on an iron bench and mopped his wounded face.

"You alright?" Lisi asked.

"I'll live," said Isaac.

"What was going on?" Lisi asked. "Why were you fighting?"

"They called me a mother's boy," said Isaac.

"Is that all?"

"It's enough!" Isaac's eyes flashed. "I am *not* a mother's boy, especially *my* mother."

"Has anything happened, Isaac?"

"Happened? Yes. My stepfather died."

"Oh, I'm sorry."

She really was. Though she didn't know it, her own troubles had given Lisi something not everyone had, true compassion.

"Well I'm not," said Isaac harshly. "Now she wants to take me away from here. She wants me to leave school and go and live with her."

"Is that so bad?"

"Bad? It's the worst thing in the world. She wants me to help with the farm. I hate farming and I don't particularly care for my mother."

Lisi wasn't sure what to say. Isaac was so full of ill-feeling, and yet he was a good-hearted boy, even if it was stifled by experience.

He softened and said, "I apologise. It's such a surprise to see you, and you caught me fighting those fools at a bad time. You never see the better side of me."

"I'm sure there is one," said Lisi, kindly.

Isaac smiled. "My mother won't bring it out,

though," he said. "I **won't** leave here. I won't go and live with her and be a farmer. I'd rather hang myself."

"Don't do that," said Lisi. "I'm sure things will work out." She waited a moment then asked, "Why don't you like your stepfather?"

Isaac had no real answer - he just didn't. The man had taken his true father's place and they had never been on the same wavelength. Isaac had a mind that wanted to understand everything whereas his stepfather had a mind that thought it already knew everything. There was no common ground. He tried explaining this to Lisi and she understood. She realised how lucky she was, in one way, having Effem and Effdee who were kind and considerate and wanted the best for her.

"What are you going to do?" she asked.

"Shout and scream till she lets me stay," he said. "Tell me something, the things I saw, were they real? I mean, are they still there?"

"Yes! Of course they are! Things don't disappear just because you can't see them."

"I know, but there was so much in such a short time, and a long time ago, for me. My head spins when I think of it all."

"You seemed to enjoy it."

"Enjoy?" Isaac dabbed his lip and said, "I was in heaven."

Lisi laughed. "It isn't heaven, it's the future, for you. I'm used to it. You could come back, if you want."

Isaac shook his head.

"I've thought of that, waited for this moment and wondered if I could go back again, but I don't think I would be allowed. Not again."

"Why not?"

"Because this is my time. I have no place there. Here, I have things to do, more now than ever. My head is filled with ideas!"

Lisi took out a clean tissue and dabbed his nose, even though it embarrassed him.

"You're very odd," she said.

Isaac sat up straight.

"And you are too. You are older than your years. Will you tell me what happened to you?"

Lisi had never spoken to anyone, but what harm could it do to tell this strange, brilliant boy whom she might never see again. She hugged her knees to her chin. For a minute she didn't say anything and Isaac thought she wasn't going to speak at all, but finally she whispered, "There was fighting."

"A fight, like that one just now?"

"No, a fight with guns."

Isaac kept very still. He felt that the mysterious girl was about to tell him something private and personal.

"Noises like thunder, all around. Explosions that deafened you if they didn't kill you. You see things on television..."

"On what?" Isaac asked.

"Doesn't matter. It isn't the same as the real thing. Nothing is. We ran but you couldn't see where to run. You couldn't see anything at all. You couldn't breathe. My mum and dad tried to keep us together but we got separated. All I remember is fear and flame and blinding lights and then a final darkness. I never saw my mum and dad again. People can be hateful," she said, "and I don't understand why."

She said it so simply, without tears or emotion, as if she was telling a story. Isaac listened, dabbing his lips.

"My parents might still be alright," said Lisi. "When I woke, I was taken away by soldiers and then everything happened so fast. A lot of children got sent away and I ended up here, I mean there," she said, "the place you saw."

"I'm sorry," said Isaac.

"That's what happens when people fight," said Lisi. "I hate it. No one wins, not really. It's the worst thing we do, and we do it over and over. Isn't that strange? Do you have wars now, Isaac?"

Isaac said they had nothing but wars, that the English had just finished the biggest civil war ever and were busy now fighting the Dutch and the Spanish.

"You see," said Lisi. "It's men mainly, they always have to find something to fight about. It goes on forever."

"You must think I make a fuss about nothing," said Isaac.

Lisi shook her head.

"What happened to me wasn't my mum or dad's fault, they didn't want it to happen."

"You mean that mine did?" Isaac asked.

Lisi didn't answer so Isaac said, "Yes, you're right. That's what makes me so angry. I can't help it you know, if I could I would be nice to everyone, but I can't be, and they don't deserve it. Come on, my nose has stopped bleeding and my lip's alright too. Come to the kitchen and I'll get you something to eat. I'm hungry after that little bout of boxing."

He led her to the school kitchen where the cooks

looked askance at Lisi but didn't seem to mind Isaac helping himself, in fact they were very friendly to him.

"They like me," he said. "Some people do."

They sat at a large wooden bench and the head cook gave them milk, bread and cheese, only it was nothing like the milk, bread and cheese she was used to. The milk was thick, the bread was thicker and the cheese could be smelt a mile away.

"Why did you come now?" Isaac asked.

"I told you, because the arch wouldn't open before."

"Why doesn't it?" asked Isaac. "I wanted to see you and your funny friend."

"It does what it does," said Lisi. "I think it does it for a reason, we just have to work out what it is."

"There are reasons for everything," said Isaac. "My stepfather said the reason is God and that was always his answer, but he was wrong. We have to find out why things are the way they are. In my head I can see the crystal you brought me. I don't suppose..."

"No," said Lisi, "sorry. It all happened too quickly."

Isaac shrugged and said, "I have my own now, not as special, but still beautiful. I can make light travel through it in different ways. And I try to remember the things I saw in your world."

"It's your world too, Isaac."

"Perhaps, one day. I feel like a caged animal, even here in school. Are your schools the same, where you can't think, you can't learn, you can't be free?"

"You make them sound like prisons," she said.

"They can be," Isaac said, "but this isn't too bad. It could be worse. There's so much I want to do, and they won't always let me. Greek and Latin, Latin and Greek until it comes out of my ears! I'm going to go to the university of Cambridge, you know. Have you heard of it?" Lisi shook her head. "I can't wait! Only... only..."

He sounded agitated.

"Only what Isaac?"

"How shall I fight my mother? She wants me to be a farmer. Me! A farmer! Never! I would hate it!"

"You hate lots of things, Isaac."

He wasn't sure whether to be angry or to laugh. He couldn't help himself and laughed out loud.

"Yes, I do. But I am not going home. I will not be a farmer! I would go mad. All those years she could have loved me but she never did, she hardly saw me, but now she needs me and I'm expected to be a good boy and do what I'm told. Well I won't!"

"Haven't you got brothers and sisters to help her?" Lisi asked.

"Yes I do," he said. "Benjamin, Mary and Hannah."

"Do you like them?" Lisi asked.

"I don't know them that well," he said, "but I think I do."

"Perhaps they can help," said Lisi.

"Yes, they will. They are her real children," said Isaac, a hint of fury returning.

Lisi touched his shoulder.

"I wish I could do something for you," she said.

Isaac suddenly looked unutterably sad and said, "You have helped me, by coming back. I wish you were my mother!"

Lisi laughed.

"I'm younger than you!" she said.

"But you would be a proper mother. You wouldn't

leave me with a grumpy old lady and run away with another man. You wouldn't ignore me until you needed me then come running for help. You aren't like that."

Lisi quite liked the idea of being Isaac's mother. He was a lonely little boy and she was, after all, three hundred years older than him.

The cook came by and stood at the table. She was a large and jolly woman with red cheeks and a nice smile.

"How are you Isaac? You look like you've been in the wars."

"I'm much better for your grub, Mrs. P. Thank you."

"Such a polite boy," she said to Lisi. "Would you like any more, young lady?"

Lisi said she couldn't eat another crumb, which was true. Even the crumbs were bigger and thicker than some of the food she was used to.

"Nice to see Isaac with a friend," said the cook. "He's a good boy, you know, one of our best, and one of our cleverest."

Isaac blushed, but he still managed to say, "I'm not one of your cleverest, Mrs. P, I'm *the* cleverest."

"So humble," laughed the cook. "And you, young lady, where are you from?"

"She's from the future, Mrs. P," said Isaac, "about three hundred years."

The cook gave a hearty laugh.

"You're a one, Mr Isaac, you really are, but I still have to throw you out. We need to do our work."

Isaac and Lisi left the kitchen and walked into the school grounds.

"I like it down there," he said. "They're kind. And they feed me more than the school."

They headed for the school gate and into town where Lisi was as fascinated as Isaac had been in London. It was so different, and she realised how shocked Isaac must have been by what he had seen. She asked him endless questions and he answered all of them. Even though his head was full of numbers and complicated problems, he knew the shop-keepers and the residents of the old town, and most of them seemed to know him.

"You're famous," she said.

"Not yet," he answered, quietly.

They got on like old friends, which in a way they were, Isaac charmed by Lisi's inquisitive mind. She wanted to know who worked in each shop, what they sold, how much things were worth, what money they used and generally how his world turned. He was glad to see her, that was clear, but he was still troubled and, when they'd covered the entire town, she knew that he wanted to talk about other things.

"What will you do?" she asked him, "if your mum says you have to leave here?"

Isaac grimaced.

"If my *mother*," he said, emphasizing how grown up he'd become, "tries to make me a farmer, I'll run away."

"Where would you go?"

"London. I shall go to London one day anyway. That's the place to live, to learn, to be famous."

"Couldn't you ask your teachers to talk with her?"

"I don't have teachers, I have one teacher, a master. Maybe. I don't know that he cares one way or the other."

"What about the headmaster?"

"Mr Stokes? What about him?"

"Couldn't you ask him to talk to her?"

123

Isaac hadn't thought about asking the school for help. He hated asking anyone for anything but perhaps he should do this. They could only say no and then he would do what he said he would do and run away.

Isaac was living with a local apothecary, a chemist who mixed medicines, some of which actually worked. Isaac helped out and found it more interesting than school which insisted on filling his head with ancient languages every second of every day.

"I'll show you," said Isaac.

It was a quaint shop, full of bottles on wooden shelves. The apothecary was an intense looking man who raised an eyebrow when he saw Lisi. Isaac introduced her as his cousin, which was fine as the apothecary's head was always elsewhere and he knew little of Isaac's family.

Isaac had a very small upstairs room, full of books, as ever. Lisi had never seen such a small room. It was just beneath the roof so the ceiling was sloped and virtually cut the room in half. His bed was a simple mattress on a wooden trestle. He wanted to show her all the things he was working on, and she did her best to look and listen, but she understood little.

"I must be quite thick," she said to him.

"Thick?" he asked.

"Foolish. To you."

"No," he said. "I'm a bad teacher."

They talked for over an hour, and though Lisi didn't follow everything Isaac said, she listened carefully and some of it actually began to make sense. She realised how much of her own life she took for granted, that despite school and books and television and a fancy computer, she didn't know that much about the way the world worked, which was one of Isaac's favourite subjects. He showed her some pictures he'd drawn of the Earth, the moon and the sun and told her how he was trying to work out why they all floated in space instead of falling down forever.

"Nothing makes sense," he said, "but I have ideas. I'd be even angrier if I didn't have ideas."

He had a misty look in his eye which made Lisi smile, he was so wrapped up in his problems. She decided that when she got home, she would Google some of them and see if she could help, though officially that would be some kind of cheat.

When it was time to leave, Isaac said again, "I really wish you were my sister. You listen to me. No one else does."

"I like you," said Lisi, " but I'm only at Key Stage Two, so I can't help you that much."

"I don't know what that means," said Isaac, "but to me you're a friend, and I haven't had a friend before. And also..."

He hesitated.

"Also what?"

"You told me something about yourself, something that means your life has been harder than mine. I'll try not to be so angry in future. It's selfish of me."

Outside, evening was falling and it was time to get back. It had been night when Lisi left her home, but night and day, never mind now and then, didn't seem to matter much to the Cabinet.

Isaac took her back to the spot where he'd been fighting the three bullies. He looked at the wall through which Lisi had popped, but that was all he saw, a solid wall. For a moment, Lisi thought she also could only see solid brick and she panicked in case she'd be stuck there forever, but then she saw the glimmering, recognisable outlines of her room. She turned to say goodbye to Isaac and was surprised to see his eyes watering.

"I'll more than likely be old when you come back again," he said. "*If* you come back again."

"I'll try to come back before you have a white beard," she said. "Good luck."

Although he was taller than her, she leaned on her tiptoes and gave him a quick kiss on the cheek. They both turned red, so it was lucky the evening was already dark.

"Bye then," she said.

"Goodbye Lisi," said Isaac, and watched as his little friend, turned, waved and vanished.

12. Orrery

The picture appeared quite suddenly and totally unexpectedly, and it appeared to Laszlo, not to Lisi. They were in Lisi's room. She'd been telling him about the last visit, that Isaac was a few years older, that his step father had died but he didn't care, that his mother wanted him to leave school and return home to be a farmer, that he was bullied and unhappy but determined.

"To do what?" Laszlo asked.

"To learn. He's so clever, Laszlo. He showed me some of the things he's been working on. It's harder than anything we do, honestly. His head is like a calculator, full of numbers. He wants to go to some place called Cambridge University."

Laszlo laughed.

"'Some place!'" he repeated. "Oxford and Cambridge are famous. Everyone knows about them."

"I didn't," said Lisi, "but that's where he wants to go. He'll do it too, I could see it in his eyes. Even if his mum tells him to come home. And he'll probably be cleverer than all the professors put together."

A week passed, and each day Lisi studied books and websites about the sun, the moon and the Earth, trying to find out what Isaac seemed to understand already.

"How does he do it?" she said to Laszlo. "He doesn't have any of this," meaning computers. "It's like he was born with it already there, in his head."

Laszlo didn't want to appear dim compared to the mysterious boy, although he couldn't think of anyone who wouldn't appear dim next to him. There was still that 'something' bothering him, as if he couldn't yet put two and two together to get four. Maybe there was nothing to put together at all, nothing to remember. But there was, he was sure of it, he just couldn't figure it out.

He was having another look at the instruction book when it happened.

"Lisi!" She turned. "Look!"

The centre pages of the manual were changing. As Laszlo slid his finger up, the arch disappeared and in its place came an assortment of footballs... no, they weren't footballs, but they were spheres, all different colours, mounted on rods poking up from other rods spreading outwards from a central hub, like the spokes of a wheel. And the instructions for making it also appeared, scrolling up and down, following Laszlo's finger.

"What is it?" he asked.

Lisi had no idea, but at the top of the page a word appeared:

ORRERY

"What is an or... or... owawee?" Laszlo asked.

Lisi put the book on her lap. The diagrams and the instructions followed her finger too.

"This reminds me of something," she said, pointing to one of the spheres. The image slowly showed more detail and colour. There was a ball in the centre of the wheel which was yellow, and nine other balls, all smaller than the one in the middle but also different sizes. The third one out was blue and green and brown.

It began to look more and more like...

"Earth!" said Laszlo.

"Yes!"

"You can see the continents. So that," he said, pointing to a red ball next to it and further out, "is Mars."

They were looking at the Solar System with the sun in the middle and the planets stretched out on wires, Mercury, Venus, Earth, Mars, Jupiter, Saturn, Uranus, Neptune and Pluto.

"Are we supposed to make this?" said Laszlo.

The cabinet doors were open and Lisi glanced at the prism. It was throbbing with light. She tapped Laszlo on the shoulder.

"I think that means 'yes'," she said.

She hadn't thought about making anything else, only the arch, but here were instructions telling her to make something called an 'Orrery'.

She moved over to the computer and searched for the word. There were about half a million explanations and she got the idea. It was simply a model of the Sun and the planets. People had used it to help figure out what was going on in the heavens.

"Why does it want us to make it?" said Laszlo, worried. "Suppose it comes to life, like the arch. You'll have the sun in your bedroom. That could be trouble."

"You have to trust it," said Lisi. "It wouldn't do anything to harm us and I'm sure it's got something to do with Isaac."

It looked quite complicated, but not impossible, and there were plenty of pieces left in the cabinet drawers. The instructions were clear, labelled one to a hundred with diagrams that slid up and down the page. You could also zoom in and out. Not easy, but do-able.

They divided the task. Lisi made the connecting rods and the hub whilst Laszlo made the planets. For these he needed curved shapes from precisely numbered drawers which fitted together to make spheres. He managed to make part of just one planet before it was time to go home. Lisi made one rod.

"Can I come back tomorrow?" Laszlo asked.

He could, and she promised not to continue by herself, which was a hard promise to keep. In fact, Laszlo came back for the next five days. Effem and Effdee asked what they were building but once again Lisi said it would be a surprise. Each evening they busied themselves. Although it was smaller than the arch, it was still fiddly. The pieces were smaller and they fitted together in a more intricate way. Each planet was made from about thirty bricks, and as ever, if they were put together the wrong way, they would glow red and you had to find correct it. You could not rush. You had to read the instructions, find the right brick in the right drawer and make sure it fitted properly, then move on.

The planets had holes in them close to their south poles. These were going to be for the spokes or rods which Lisi was building. They were more delicate than the planets, like a spider-web with each strand made from parallel rows of bricks joined by struts. They weren't supposed to fit the planets to the rods until the very end, and when they tried, the bricks not only glowed red but fell apart.

It wasn't easy to talk while they worked because they were concentrating so hard, but now and again they took a break.

"What do you think this is for?" Lisi asked as she set down a pair of rods on her bed.

"We'll find out soon enough," said Laszlo. "I bet it has something to do with him," he said, nodding at the ivory arch, standing silent and innocent in Lisi's bedroom. This was true, but what was it the instructions said:

To meet one who has gone before
And left their mark for evermore

Isaac had been and gone, and been again for a few hours, but what mark had he left? That was a mystery. Did it have something to do with this orrery they were building? If she got a chance, Lisi would take it through, though by that time the unhappy boy might well be an unhappy man. Time shifted about quite unpredictably on the other side of the arch.

"There's a reason," said Lisi, "we can't see it yet."

"There's something else I can't see," said Laszlo. "It's been bothering me for ages."

"What?" asked Lisi.

"Well that's it, I don't know what!" said Laszlo. "It's like I heard something important and missed it, now I can't remember what it was."

"To do with the cabinet?"

"No, him. Your friend."

"He's your friend too."

"Okay, but it's something to do with him."

Whatever it was, Laszlo couldn't make the connection. Isaac was a clever, troubled boy, but why he should be singled out for their visits they didn't know, and why Lisi should have been singled out to win the cabinet in the first place they didn't know either.

The orrery was coming along nicely. Most exciting was when they started fitting the planets to the rods. There were nine upright rods joined to the horizontal spokes and each planet sat on one of these rods, but there were also small supporting rods to make sure they didn't fall off. What puzzled them was that there was no mechanism. There didn't seem to be a way that the planets could revolve around the sun, so it had to be a fixed model. That was disappointing. It would have been interesting to see the whole thing work like the real solar system.

The planets were tricky but the sun was more so, even though the planets had seas and land and mountains and all kinds of interesting features whereas the sun was a ball of gas. Laszlo, who was doing the planets and sun by himself, had trouble with it, probably because the pieces were so similar, all two hundred of them. And yet it wasn't solid. There was a space inside for something, and they knew what that something was. The prism.

The instructions were clear. When the orrery was almost finished, you put the prism inside the two halves of the sun. About three quarters of the way through making it, Laszlo tried it. It looked like it would fit okay, but nothing happened.

"Perhaps it lights up," he said.

"Or goes around," said Lisi, though they couldn't see how it could possibly do that.

Lisi placed Mercury on its support. It had taken six

days to get that far but it was worth waiting for as it gave them a good idea of how the other planets would look. They wanted to hurry but they had to take their time, step by tiny step. If they got tired and tried to do too much, the instructions wouldn't scroll down so they didn't know what to do, and there was no way of guessing.

They finished on a Sunday evening, Laszlo sitting on Lisi's bed with the prism in his hands, the orrery on the floor and Lisi kneeling next to it, admiring their work. It was about a metre in diameter but the horizontal spokes were hinged so it could fold, not with special metal hinges but in the clever way the bricks fitted together. The whole thing could be folded along each of the nine spokes into a kind of octopus shape and stored neatly with the sun at the bottom and the planets squidged together, still mounted on the rods.

"It's so clever," said Laszlo. "And beautiful, even if I say so myself. I wonder who designed it?"

Wonder as they might, they had no answer. If Mr Angel had designed it, he was a mighty clever man wasting his time managing an amusement arcade.

"Shall we?" said Lisi, nodding towards the prism and the sun.

All the bricks were in place, the only thing left to do was put the prism inside the sun which was hinged into two halves with a hole in the middle.

They hesitated because they were afraid nothing would happen. The arch had led them through to the past, and the past back to their present, so what would this model do?

"Maybe we should call Laura and Adam to come and

see," said Laszlo.

They'd been brilliant giving her all this time and trust so perhaps Lisi ought to share this with them. They were delighted to visit 'The Den' as they called Lisi's bedroom. She hadn't let them in since she and Laszlo had started the second model so they were expecting something equally magnificent.

When they saw the spidery shape spread out in the centre of the floor, they were intrigued. Lisi was going to tell them what it was but Adam said, "It's an orrery!" which impressed everyone.

"It's ingenious!" said Laura.

"It isn't finished," Lisi explained. "We have to put the prism inside the sun."

"To make it do what?" Adam asked.

They didn't know. The only way was to try it and see.

Laszlo carefully placed the prism in the sun and closed the curved hinged door to seal it in.

Many things could have happened. When you have a Cabinet of Wonders, fantastic things do happen, but sometimes very ordinary things happen, or even nothing at all. It all depends on what it has in mind. This time, it seemed to have very little in mind.

The sun and the planets started to glow, each with the colours of the real sun and planets. They weren't exact, but you knew what they were supposed to be, so Earth was blue with shades of green and brown, Mars mainly red, Venus a misty yellow, but all the colours were pale shadows of the true, deep hues of the actual planets. The whole thing was clever, but a touch disappointing.

"Very nice," said Laura. "Does it do anything else?"

They were all hoping for something more

spectacular, especially Lisi and Laszlo who knew what the cabinet could do, if it had a mind to do so.

"Perhaps you could hang it from the ceiling," said Laura, "as a mobile. It would look nice."

"It's a bit heavy for that," said Lisi. "We'll think of something. I don't want to take it apart yet. It was quite hard to make."

Effem and Effdee looked again at the arch standing noble and proud, splitting Lisi's bedroom in half.

"And this?" Laura asked.

Lisi hadn't told them the truth about the arch because as sure as eggs were eggs they wouldn't believe her. She sighed and said, "Yes, we'll take that down too, soon."

They didn't dismantle the orrery, not having put so much effort into making it. Instead they folded it up and put it into a plastic department store bag, removing the prism from the Sun and placing it back in the cabinet.

Over the next few days, Lisi occasionally opened it out and put the prism back in, seeing if anything different would happen, but it didn't. The sun and planets glowed their pale, unimpressive colours, but that was all.

"You're not ready," she whispered, half to the orrery and half to herself, "are you?"

It wasn't, not until three weeks had passed. Laszlo had come round for tea and they were doing some homework together when the arch sprang into life.

It was remarkably sudden, as if someone had flicked a switch. Lights rolled around it like a liquid rainbow. The wall behind the arch vanished and instead there was both a familiar and unfamiliar sight.

"Hurry!" Lisi whispered. "The prism!"

Laszlo took it from the cabinet whilst Lisi grabbed the bag.

"Ready?" she asked.

Laszlo wasn't sure if she was asking him, the orrery, the arch or the dark figure within, so he didn't say anything, just nodded quickly and followed her once again into the past.

13. The University of Cambridge

A young man was peering intently at a book resting on an oak desk in a small study. Around him were the signs of an academic life, more books, quills and parchments and various scientific and mathematical pieces of equipment. The man had dark hair and a fearsomely determined expression. Even though he was stooping, the children could see that he was not much taller than Laszlo, about five feet six inches. He didn't hear them approach through the panelled fireplace in his study and continued to stare at his book.

"Hello Isaac."

The young man looked up and, after a moment of shock, his fearsome expression changed to one of delight.

"Lisi?"

"Yes. And Laszlo."

"Good Heavens! You haven't changed at all!"

"You have. You're all grown up."

"Not all grown up, but five years have passed. I'm nineteen now!"

Isaac threw his arms around the girl and shook hands with Laszlo who blushed, both with embarrassment and confusion. Five years!

"I'm still thirteen," said Lisi.

"How long?" Isaac asked.

"Oh, just a few weeks."

Isaac shook his head in amazement. He pointed to all his books and said, "I am considered clever here at Cambridge. Indeed, I consider myself clever, but this defeats me. I don't understand how you do it."

"Neither do we," said Lisi. "I'm glad that you're here though," she said. "I thought we might find you farming with your mother."

Isaac looked puzzled for a moment, then said, "Ah, that! No, it all worked out."

"How?" Lisi asked.

"How? Well, I did go back for a while, but I was as unhappy as a boy could be. Then the headmaster of The King's School offered to take me into his home."

"Mr Stokes?" Lisi asked.

"Yes! You remember! He changed my life, Lisi. He let me stay with him and study at the school."

Lisi and Laszlo tried to imagine their headmistress letting them stay with her but they couldn't. It was more far-fetched than time-travel.

"This isn't the school any more, is it?" Laszlo asked, looking around.

"No, my boy! This is Cambridge University!"

Laszlo found it odd to be called 'my boy' by the young man who had been a boy with him not so long ago. So much had changed.

"Let me look at you!" said Isaac, and there were tears in his eyes as he held Lisi by the shoulders and admired her, then the same with Laszlo. "I really thought I'd dreamed it all," he said. "I told myself it couldn't have been real because there was no explanation for it except my unhappy state of mind. I thought you were a figment of my imagination."

"I'm not," said Lisi. "I'm me."

"And I'm me," said Laszlo.

"Of course you are," said Isaac. "And I am still me, despite being slightly taller."

"Not that much," said Lisi, and Isaac laughed.

"I am no giant," he said, "but I have stood on the shoulders of giants." The children looked puzzled. "To learn what I have learned," said Isaac. "For anyone to learn, they must stand on the shoulders of those who have lived before them to see the truth. And I have stood on the shoulders of many great thinkers, Ptolemy, Copernicus, Kepler."

Lisi and Laszlo had never heard of any of them and they shook their heads, feeling rather stupid.

"You'll learn of them in time," said Isaac. "And others. But you know the person who raised me the highest?" They didn't. "You," he said to Lisi.

"Me?"

"Yes," said Isaac, more enthusiastic than Lisi ever remembered him. "You were my friend when I had no friends. You gave me guidance when I had none. You gave me hope when I had no hope."

"Did I?" Lisi asked.

"You did, and you both showed me something wonderful, the future."

They remembered the trip to the museum, but it was just a few hours out for them. For Isaac, it had shaped his life when it was falling apart.

"Did you like it?" Laszlo asked.

Isaac laughed.

"Like it? I was dumbfounded. I saw things that even I can't fathom, not even now. We take tiny steps forward, even in a hundred years, just a few steps, but you took me great leaps forward, and I could barely cope. I was unwell for days."

"Sorry!" said Lisi.

"Oh no, not your fault, and I was unwell with amazement, not ill health. It was like eating too much food or drinking too much wine. And seeing you now, it all comes back to me, those startling visions! And you see them every day!"

"You get used to it," said Laszlo.

"But I had no time," said Isaac. "Before I could take in anything, I was back here, and I have spent years trying to unravel the mysteries. I fear I will spend the next years unravelling them too, and still not succeed, but I will do my best. How strange it is to see you again after all this time. Come in properly, see my home!"

He ushered them into his study which wasn't really his home, but as he spent most of his day there, it felt like it. He ordered a servant to fetch some drinks and cakes for his guests.

"You have a servant!" said Laszlo, impressed.

"Not just mine. He works here at Trinity."

"Trinity?" Lisi asked.

"The College."

"I thought you said this is Cambridge."

"It is Trinity College Cambridge! The world knows of it! Look," said Isaac, leading them to the window.

They peered out and could tell they were in some grand tower. Outside were more buildings and a lush courtyard.

"This reminds me of when I looked out of your window in your bedroom."

"So long ago," said Isaac.

"Not for me," said Lisi.

"No, but years past for me," Isaac said, wistfully. "So hard to understand, despite all my studies."

There was a little awkward silence, because as friendly as they were to each other now, they realised that there was an awful gap in knowledge. To the children, Isaac felt like some mighty wizard who knew everything there was to know, whilst to him the children felt like... well, like children. He was aware suddenly how much he had grown and changed. A bleak expression passed across his face, as if remembering his unhappy days as a boy had caused the terrible moods to return.

"Are you alright?" Lisi asked. "You didn't mind us coming, did you?"

"Mind? No! Never! I just... I just recall my anger and bitterness. It hasn't left me, Lisi, it never will, but it drives me!"

"You're quite scary," she said. "You used to be when you were small, but you're more now."

Isaac smiled bravely, but the mood couldn't quite leave him.

"I can be a monster," he said, "but a good hearted one."

Laszlo was looking at some of the books. They were way too hard for him to understand, and some were in foreign languages, though not Polish.

"Do you like it here?" he asked.

Isaac didn't answer straight away. He thought for a moment then said, "I would not be anywhere else, but at the same time, I wish it would change."

"Why?" asked Lisi.

"Because these men of learning," he said, swishing his arm out to cover all of Cambridge, "know only one thing, their precious ancient world, the world of Greece and Rome. And it is precious, but it isn't all there is. There is more, much, much more. You know that and I know that, but they don't. They are stuck in the past. They cannot think new thoughts. They think only what other men have taught them to think. I cannot bear it sometimes."

"You can teach them, can't you?" said Lisi.

Isaac was delighted at this.

"I can and I will, little Lisi," he said. "I have plans to stay here, ruffle a few feathers, shake the old place up a bit. Would you like a tour? Shall I show you this most famous building?"

Isaac was a good guide this time, and his colleagues were astonished to see him smiling, accompanied by children who, as a rule, he avoided. Lisi and Laszlo felt the importance of the university. It seemed to seep through the old stone walls and up through the even older stone floors. But they both felt uncomfortably small next to the massive stone buildings.

On the lawn outside Trinity College, Isaac said, "I have memories of your world, but it is like a dream to me, so many strange and wonderful things. This must be dull for you."

"Not dull," said Lisi, "but it's a bit... a bit..."

"Miserable," said Laszlo.

Lisi gave him a look as if he'd made an embarrassing mistake, but Isaac agreed.

"Yes, it can be," he said, "but I work well here. This

is, and will be, my home for many years."

"Will you be happy?" Lisi asked.

Isaac's features darkened in that sudden, fearful way they'd seen before, but he wasn't angry with them, he was angry at something inside himself.

"I am never happy," he said. "I wish I could be, but I never was. Only moments. I am happy to see you both."

"And we're happy to see you," said Laszlo. "We brought you something."

"The prism?" said Isaac, expectantly. "I have dreamed about it, you know. It meant everything to me. There was so much knowledge hidden inside it, so much to learn from it! Is that the present you've brought me?"

"Yes and no," said Lisi. "Can we go back to your room? We can't take it out here."

On the way back, Isaac told them of his time with the apothecary and with Mr Stokes. He told them about the things he had done and the things he was going to do. He asked them what they were doing and if their world was still as mad as ever, and if the museum was still there too.

"Everything is still there," said Lisi. "Just the same. It's only been a few months, remember."

"Astonishing, astonishing," muttered Isaac.

When they arrived back in his room, they asked Isaac to clear a space on his desk. Then Laszlo took the department store bag, which was fascinating in itself to Isaac, and placed the closed orrery in the middle. Isaac stared at it, then at the children, then touched the folded rods.

"Is it dangerous?" he asked.

"No! It's beautiful," said Lisi. "We made it. And I

suppose we made it for you, though we didn't know it while we were doing it."

"So what exactly is it?" Isaac asked.

"We'll show you," said Laszlo.

He and Lisi slowly opened out the orrery, spreading the horizontal spokes, raising the vertical rods and making sure the planets were all in position. Isaac had never seen such a thing and his brows were furrowed as he tried to fathom what it would do.

"This is the sun and the planets," he said. "I can see that. It is clever. But..."

"Wait," said Laszlo. "It needs this."

He took out the prism and Isaac gasped.

"Let me see it!" he said.

Laszlo gave it to Isaac who held it high and gazed into its heart.

"My friend!" he said to the crystal. "Here you are again! Now will you tell me your secrets?"

They let him hold it and inspect it again, as he'd dreamed of doing since he'd first seen it years before.

"It's the battery," said Laszlo.

"The what?"

"The battery. It makes the model... well, wait and see."

Isaac gave the prism back to Laszlo who put it into the heart of the sun. Isaac watched, spellbound.

"I hope you're not disappointed," said Lisi. "We were, a little, but it's still very nice."

The sun and planets began to glow and Isaac took a step back. His age had no batteries, no portable power at all, so this was unheard of. Light from nothing! And such colours!

"Are the planets truly these colours?" he asked.

"We think so," said Lisi.

"And so many of them!" said Isaac.

"Just the normal number," said Laszlo.

Isaac knew only of six, including Earth, but who was he to argue with two children from a mysterious future? He had to believe what he was seeing, which was the most astonishing thing he had ever seen!

"It didn't do that before," whispered Lisi.

"No, it definitely didn't," said Laszlo.

The sun was brighter and the planet colours deeper, but more than this, the whole orrery had begun to turn.

"You made this?" Isaac asked. "It is... wondrous!"

"The book showed us how to make it," said Laszlo, "but it never turned before."

"And it definitely never did that!" said Lisi.

Very slowly, the orrery lifted itself and floated a millimetre or so above the wooden surface of the table.

"How...?" Isaac began to say, but he stopped, entranced by the show which was changing, moment by moment.

Next, each planet began to turn on its axis, not fast, but noticeably so, all except Mercury which faced the same way as it turned around the ever brighter sun.

The three watchers thought that would be all, but the orrery hadn't finished its show, not by a long way.

The spokes and rods started to fade, as if an invisible hand was rubbing them out. In a minute, they had all vanished, and the spinning planets turned around the spinning sun, held by nothing at all!

"Honestly, Isaac," said Lisi, who saw her friend staring with disbelief and wonder, "it never did this before!"

The light from the window had faded as the light from the orrery sun brightened. In a few moments the room was dark and the solar system hovered above Isaac's desk like some magical projection.

"I am not scared," said Isaac. "I am never scared. But I am... I am... in awe!"

He peered at each planet, even put his hand in the plane of the gently turning wheel, his mind buzzing with ideas. How? Why? A thousand questions needed to be answered and he determined to answer as many of them as he could.

"Something!" Lisi and Laszlo heard him mutter the word. "Something holds them there!" he said. "Some... force holds it all together."

"The prism," said Laszlo. "It must be."

"No!" said Isaac. "Your beautiful prism holds this wonderful model, but in the true heavens, something makes this system work! There is no prism in the sun, Laszlo."

Lisi caught a glimpse of Isaac's face. It was glowing in the dark room, alive with exhilaration and intelligence. He was as close to the truth as he had ever been, but not yet close enough. His eyes sparkled with wonder and delight, and Lisi almost laughed to see this clever man so caught up in the model she'd brought to show him, even if it was doing more than it had ever done for her.

"The sun, the sun!" he said. "I can hardly look at it!"

The sun was fiercely bright. It held the planets in thrall, casting its light on them.

"Look!" said Laszlo. "Moons! I didn't make them,

Lisi!"

There were moons not just around Earth, but around most of the other planets, and some planets had an extraordinary number. Nor were they made of the cabinet's bricks, they were real moons, all colours, all shapes, and some even spouting fire.

"Impossible!" said Isaac.

The whole thing was impossible, and yet they could see so much detail of every planet and every moon.

"Do you like it?" Lisi asked.

"Like it! It is the most beautiful thing in the world... beyond the world. There are no words..." he started to say, but he was almost crying with enjoyment. "I must... I must think about this..."

He walked around the magical vision, never taking his eye off the orrery now floating at least a metre above the table, studying every detail, his brain in overdrive. There were things at work here that baffled him – almost everything about it baffled him, but he knew this was a chance to learn, and there was nothing that he needed so much in life as to learn how the universe worked.

Lisi and Laszlo were equally fascinated. Neither of them had expected such a magnificent display from their orrery. Lisi was almost laughing at the beauty of it whilst Laszlo realised just how much he didn't know. There he was thinking himself a clever boy, but he didn't understand why the sun and all the planets could float like that, not in the model but in real life. He'd seen images of the solar system in countless television programmes, but if anyone had asked him, he wouldn't have known why the sun and planets did what they did. Why didn't they all fall down? How come they kept on spinning and didn't slow down? How was it they didn't all smash into each other? He had no idea, but he would definitely look into it when he got back.

Isaac was thinking along the same lines. For thousands of years people had looked at the sky with the naked eye and tried to understand what they saw, like why stars moved so slowly but planets wandered around in such a hurry. The very word 'planet' meant 'wanderer' to ancient peoples who made up endless stories about the patterns of light they saw in the night sky. Isaac knew what they knew, and he knew that almost everything they believed was wrong.

"Yes!" he whispered to himself, "that must be why..." and "The force here could be... hmm, I must measure that..." and "I wonder if we could see more closely if... yes, that would work!"

It was as if he was having a hundred conversations with himself at once. Lisi wanted to speak but was afraid of disturbing him. She remembered how hard she'd seen him concentrate when he was a boy, and his face had exactly the same expression now, fully focused. Nothing would distract him. She knew now that the orrery had been made as much for Isaac as for her and Laszlo, but she still couldn't believe what it was doing! Was it magic? Was it science? Was it a bit of both? Did Mr Angel at the seaside amusement arcade know that it would do this? She had so many questions too, but she was also as caught up in the wonder of the moment as the others. She doubted that she would ever see anything so lovely again.

Slowly, the light from the orrery sun started to fade and the natural light in Isaac's room returned. The spinning planets stopped spinning, the orrery stopped turning, the colours dimmed and the whole solar system sank back onto the table.

Isaac, Lisi and Laszlo were left staring at the still and silent model, none of them wanting to break the mood of wonder. At last, Lisi whispered, "Isaac? Are you alright?"

Isaac's cheeks were flushed and his eyes watering. He looked transformed into something beyond the clever, handsome young man that he undoubtedly was.

"You have shown me something... magnificent!" he said. "I don't know how I shall ever thank you!"

"You don't have to," said Lisi, "but we'd better go now."

"You are taking this... this wonderful model with you?"

"I have to," said Lisi.

Isaac nodded, but he was so unwilling to let it be taken away. Lisi took out the prism and put it on the table, then folded up the orrery and put it into the department store bag. So curious, she thought, that she could put all that wonder into something so flimsy. Isaac watched her.

"I will repay you somehow," he said. "You have freed me, Lisi and Laszlo."

"Freed you?"

"Yes. I was puzzling over so much. I was almost in a prison of despair wondering if I would ever find the answers, but you have given me ideas, rare and precious ideas."

"I hope they're good ones," said Laszlo.

"Let me have one more look at the prism," said Isaac,

picking it up and inspecting it. "I doubt I will ever see it again," he said.

"We might be back," said Lisi. "You never know. It's a funny thing, this cabinet. Very unpredictable."

"I hope we meet again," said Isaac, "but if not, I want to remember this," he said, studying the prism, "and that," he said, pointing at the bag, "but most important, I want to remember you two," he said, and put a hand on each of their shoulders.

"We'll remember you too," said Lisi. "Always."

They headed towards the panelled archway through which they could see Lisi's bedroom in a swirl of mist.

"You could come with," said Lisi, "if you hold my hand," but Isaac shook his head.

"This is my home, my time, and I have things to do. Goodbye Laszlo. Goodbye Lisi."

"We might be allowed through again tomorrow," said Lisi, "it just happens."

Isaac smiled. "Somehow I doubt it," he said. "You have shown me how to see things differently. You always did. Perhaps you can also see things differently and be happy, little Lisi."

"I'm alright," said Lisi.

"I think you will be yet more alright," laughed Isaac, which was a lovely thing to say, and still ringing in Lisi's ears as she and Laszlo headed back into the twenty-first century, waving to the mysterious dark-eyed young man they'd left behind.

14. Letters

A year after her first visit and longer since she lay in the garden talking to the cloud, Lisi was there again, only this time she had the prism with her. It had become something of a comfort, letting her see the world in a different way. She was laying on the grass, looking through it at anything that came into her line of vision, fascinated by the reflections and refractions of colour.

She couldn't remember how she felt a year ago, but she hoped she was happier and a little wiser. That might have been because Laszlo was a friend or it might have been because she'd met Isaac who seemed to carry the weight of the world and all its knowledge on his shoulders. She wasn't sure, but she hoped that she was growing up the right way, whatever that meant.

The prism helped in its own small way. When she looked through it, her unhappiness dissolved, as if the prism could split it into tiny pieces which didn't matter. It split everything except the things she could see in its heart, if only she could work out what they were.

She sometimes tried walking with the prism in front of her but it made her giddy. Other times she counted the colours. There seemed to be far more colours inside the prism than out, which meant that it was showing her things that she couldn't see without it. Clearly, the patterns deep inside were important but she still didn't know what they meant, but if understanding was easy, it wouldn't be worth much. Truth was often hard to find.

She turned the prism one way, then another, studying the colours and the shapes that were impossible to see without it. She hoped it might show her Isaac to see what he was up to, but it didn't. Nevertheless, she wondered about him and hoped he was alright. She saw multiple blues from the sky and greys and whites from the clouds. She saw dozens of greens from the grass and had looked up the internet to find names for them, like emerald, lime, myrtle, fern, forest, shamrock, harlequin and jungle. She didn't know which was which, but there were enough shades to go around, and more besides. When she put the crystal down and the world came together again, the shades remained, for a while.

She never forgot what had happened, but looking through the prism made it more real. She had told Isaac a little about herself and felt better for talking to him. Looking through the prism did the same thing. She could never forget the fighting she had seen with all its madness, but there was such peace within the prism, a truth there that couldn't be touched by the violence of men.

She turned onto her tummy and looked into the crystal with the sun behind her. It magnified the grass and let her see in between the blades. A few scurrying ants when magnified looked scarily huge. She wondered if they could see her and what they would make of her giant eye peering at them.

If she was perfectly still, she thought she could indeed see Isaac, but it was only her imagination. She didn't know how old he would be if she ever managed to get back to him. Weeks here had been years there, so months here might be forever there! Poor boy. She felt so sorry for him, especially when she'd first met him, but he seemed to be surer of himself and maybe she'd helped a little.

She and Laszlo were both far more into discovering things than before, which was a major effect of their time hopping. They did funny experiments together, like making racing boats out of squeezy bottles, talking through tin and string telephone lines, mixing bubbles, making bridges out of paper, powering tiny electric motors, making crystal radios, growing a chemical garden and magnifying the rays of the sun. They wondered if Isaac would be impressed or laugh at them.

She was feeling sleepy and almost dropping off when she heard Effem's voice.

"Letter, Lisi. I think it might be important."

She sat up. She never got letters, only emails, and they were from Laszlo telling her a new experiment he wanted to carry out. She stood as Laura brought out an official looking letter. It was in a brown envelope, long and narrow, with an embassy stamp on the front. Her name was printed in very neat letters, but it was her original name, not Effem's and Effdee's name.

"You can open it now," said Effem looking a little nervous, "or wait till Adam gets back. It's up to you, sweetheart."

Laura had seen the embassy postmark and guessed that the letter had something to do with Lisi's past. She also guessed that if it was something bad, the embassy would have written to her and Adam as they were Lisi's guardians. If it was something good, then she could understand them writing to Lisi, and Effem dearly wanted good news for the girl. She and Adam did not want to lose her but they wanted the best for her. They had never had a child of their own and they loved Lisi so much, it would break their hearts to see her go.

"I'll wait," said Lisi.

She also saw the embassy postmark and was nervous too, but she wanted both her foster parents there when she opened the letter.

Adam arrived in the evening and they sat around the dining table as quiet as mice. The atmosphere was filled with expectation and dread at the same time.

"Thank you for waiting," said Adam. "I appreciate it. You can open the letter now, Lisi. You must."

"It's probably nothing," Lisi said.

"Maybe. Only one way to find out," said Adam.

Lisi studied the letter again for a moment then carefully slid her finger through the sticky flap. She peered inside first, as if she could read the folded letter, took it out, flattened it on the table and stared at it.

The embassy address was printed along the top of the paper in a beautiful script. Beneath it was Lisi's name and address and then the following letter which Lisi read aloud:

Dear Lisi,
We have some wonderful news for you. Your mother and father have been found and are safe and well. Both were captive for over a year but have been released along with a number of other prisoners. They were hurt in the fighting where they lost track of you but their wounds have healed, they are in good

health and are desperate to see you again. If you and your guardians could call us as soon as possible, we will arrange a reunion. We are all very happy for you at the embassy and look forward to seeing you.

Regards...

and it was signed by the ambassador to Lisi's homeland.

She kept looking at the letter after she'd finished reading it then became aware that Effem and Effdee had said nothing. She looked up and saw them holding hands.

"They're alive," said Lisi.

Laura got up and hugged her foster daughter.

"I'm so happy for you, Lisi. We both are."

"I'll have to go back," she said.

She said this with mixed feelings. She'd been in England a long time and it felt like the safest, loveliest place on Earth. How could she go back to the place of nightmares where hatred had taken over and killing replaced loving? But how could she not? It was her true home and where she belonged. And her parents were alive! After all she had seen and believed, they were alive!

"What should I do?" she asked in such a pitiful way that Effem and Effdee almost burst into tears.

"Call them now, or first thing tomorrow morning," said Adam, checking his watch. "Your parents are alive, Lisi. That's a miracle."

Yes, it was a miracle, and she longed to see them. So why did she also feel a little trepidation and even sadness? Because Effem and Effdee had been so good to her and she didn't want to lose them. Maybe they could all live together. Her parents could come here and they could start again in England. They wouldn't want to stay where there was still so much danger, would they?

"Will you come with me?" she asked.

"Of course, love!" said Laura, "as if we would pack you off all by yourself!"

"I mean back... home," said Lisi.

"We'll do whatever you want," said Laura.

For some reason, Lisi heard Isaac's voice in her head, '*I suppose your mother and father are behind the arch, waiting for you to come back into their loving arms.*' Well, he had sorted himself out and she would sort herself out too. She wondered what he would say. Despite being madly clever, he was generous hearted and kind. He would be happy for her happiness as much as Effem and Effdee, and maybe Laszlo too, but he wouldn't want to see her go.

That evening, Laura sat on her bed and they spoke.

"You know we're delighted for you," she said.

"I might have to leave you," said Lisi.

"There's no 'might' about it," said Laura, "you *will* have to leave us. But we'll stay in touch, one way or the other. You'll never really leave us."

She glanced across at the arch which had been a feature of Lisi's bedroom for so long that Laura had almost forgotten it was there.

"Will you take that with you?" she asked.

Lisi didn't know what to say. She couldn't take it with so she would have to take it down, but not yet. Not quite yet.

"Things happened," she said. "I'm not making it up. They did."

Now Lisi was the most sensible girl in the world and Laura found this a strange thing for her to say.

"What things, Lisi?"

"That boy," said Lisi, "the one you met who came with us to the museum? I met him in there," she said, pointing to the arch. "He's still there."

This upset Laura. Lisi was clever and sensible, so why would she say such an odd thing? If she hadn't met the boy herself, she would have been even more doubtful, but she had met him and he was truly the oddest boy she had ever seen. He was very much like a child taken out of time, alone and vulnerable.

"Can I meet him again?" said Laura.

"It doesn't work like that," said Lisi. "It only lets us see him when it feels like it or when it's the right time."

Laura almost said that Lisi was too old to make up stories, but she already felt that she was no longer Lisi's mother, not even her foster mother. She wasn't Effem now, she was plain old Laura. She didn't say anything but kissed the girl on the forehead and said goodnight.

Lisi didn't go to sleep. She sat her desk, took out a pen and paper and wrote a letter, one she realised she had to write:

"Dear Mr Angel,

I know you'll think that I'm ungrateful, but I'm not. It's been the best time of my life having the cabinet in my bedroom. I won't tell you what I made with it because you won't believe me, but what I'm thinking now is that I should give it back to you. I've been thinking this for a few days. It's probably the only one of its kind. I definitely can't imagine another one like it. If that's true, then someone else might like to have it. I think that it's done what it's supposed to do for me and for someone called Isaac and for Laszlo. Neither of them were my friends before I won the jackpot, so maybe the jackpot was them, not the cabinet, if you see what I mean. They are both special people.

I can't see what else I can build that would make a difference. You see, I had a letter today telling me that my mother and father are alive and coming to the Embassy here to meet me. This probably has nothing to do with the cabinet, but since it has been here, unusual things have happened. Even if I kept the cabinet for a hundred years, I don't think it could do anything more unusual than what it's done already.

I am sure that there's someone out there like me who needs it, and I won't mind giving it to them. It would be selfish to keep it longer. Lots of people give things away to charity shops or sell them, but I can't do this with my jackpot prize, it's too special. I would much rather give it back to you so that you can make it a prize for someone else. Is that alright?

Another reason is that probably, when I meet my real mum and dad again, I will have to go home with them, and the cabinet is too big to take with me. I have to take down what I've made but then please could you come and collect it from me? I will be sorry to say goodbye to it, it's part of my bedroom, part of me, but this isn't going to be my bedroom much longer.

Thank you very much for bringing it here. Such a long time ago! I know you won't mind having it back to give to another lucky winner.

Yours sincerely,
Lisi

Lisi read the letter through, folded it, and addressed it to Mr Angel. She put it on her bedside table then climbed into bed and lay on her side for a while, facing the arch.

She thought about all the things that had happened during the year and most of all about the letter she'd received that day. Her heart was full to overflowing. A while ago she had no one at all in her life, everything had been torn away. Now she had a real friend in Laszlo, a dream friend in Isaac and four parents – two mothers and two fathers, all loving, all wanting the best for her. That beat any jackpot, hands down.

She closed her eyes, more at peace with the world than she'd been for a long, long time.

15. The Royal Society

Sir Isaac Newton stood at the front of the lecture theatre in the Royal Society. The year was 1710 and Newton was sixty-eight years old. He was as much a puzzle to himself as to the extraordinary people seated in front of him, listening with rapt attention. They were extraordinary because they were the brightest of the bright, the best natural philosophers or scientists of their time and Newton was the best of the best. He was their president, The President of the Royal Society. It sounded grand because it was grand, not in an empty celebrity way, but in an astonishingly clever way.

He had discovered so much in his life, and he was still busy even at sixty-eight. He had pushed the boundaries of knowledge forward in many areas of learning, any one of which might have made him President of The Royal Society. He wasn't particularly liked because he was a little scary, but he was respected because of all that he had done.

The Royal Society had been around for about fifty years and had just moved to a new and plush home. This was one of the first lectures there and the place was filled with a sense of excitement and hope. They were excited because learning anything new about the world is exciting, and Newton had found out more about it than anyone in history. He was modest enough to say that many clever people before him had done their bit, but he also knew how hard he had worked and what he had achieved. Most people were in awe of him. It didn't seem normal for one person to have found out so much about so many things, but he'd done just that, month after month, year after year, all his life.

No one knew him, except perhaps his step brother and sisters who remembered what he'd been like as a boy, but even then, they said, he'd been a puzzle – intense, angry and desperate to learn. No one could tell him what to do or how to live. He was fiercely determined and wildly intelligent, separate from his fellow men, driven by something deep and strong which no one understood.

He had told the world about light, about mathematics and about gravity. He had thought about the universe in a new way and come up with countless new ideas. He was, in short, a genius, and there was no one else who could have been President of The Royal Society at this historic time but Isaac Newton.

What was going on in his mind as he faced the best and brightest minds of the generation no one knew, not even Newton himself. Friends hoped he might be happier, but no matter what he achieved, nothing cheered him. He looked partly sad, partly ferocious as he spoke to his audience who hung on his every word. Some were jealous. They wished they knew what he knew or had done what he'd done, but many were simply respectful, knowing that he was different, and that made him more interesting. He was what he was and did not care for what he could never be. There was little room in his mind for happiness nor much for love, but he was still a kind and good man, which was surprising seeing as though he had, rightly or wrongly, felt abandoned his entire life.

He was a good speaker, always interesting, but there came a moment during his talk when he stopped still, fell silent and just stared at the back wall. The audience wondered if he was unwell, but he seemed to be fine, just puzzlingly preoccupied. They wondered too if he had suddenly come up with a new idea. They knew that he was working on a massively clever book so perhaps he'd been thinking about it for a moment and forgotten to speak. There was silence in the hall. Someone coughed, and then someone else, very brave, whispered, "Sir Isaac, are you alright?" He didn't answer, but a strange smile appeared on his face. Newton rarely smiled and this caused whispers of unrest in the audience. None present could ever guess, though, not in a million revolutions of the Earth around the sun.

Set in the wooden wainscoting of the wall was an arch and this reminded him of something he hadn't seen for many years. He had begun to wonder if what he remembered had happened at all. His head was full of wonders and this was a particularly odd one which he feared might have been the result of feverish imaginings brought on by tiredness and overwork. Anything real could be proved. You did this with experiments, but as hard as he had tried, he had never solved the puzzle of the arch and its visitors.

What caught his attention was not the shape, but what, for a few fleeting moments, he thought he saw beyond it. Seeing anything beyond a solid wall was surprising enough, especially as he himself had done so much work on light that he knew it to be impossible, but the wooden panelled arch had appeared to fade.

Newton blinked and stared.

Something was happening, but what?

People in the audience turned to look, but all they saw was a dark brown wooden panelled arch set in the back wall of the lecture theatre. They became restless, hoping that the great man hadn't gone mad. That happened sometimes, people suddenly losing their way, befuddled by their own brains. It was frightening, but even more so when it happened to someone as clever as this.

But it hadn't happened. He was still the man he had been, only now the audience was astonished to see a tiny tear in his eye. Newton shedding a tear was like the sun turning blue - it never happened, and they couldn't explain it. He told them afterwards that a speck of dust had plagued him, but this was one truth that he wouldn't tell anyone.

Beyond the panel, a white room was visible, full of strange equipment. A young man and a young woman were hunched over machines, engrossed. The young man looked up with an expression of surprise, as if he had finally solved a lifelong problem. He smacked his head as if incredulous of his own stupidity and mouthed something to the woman who looked up. Newton knew them both, older, wiser and cleverer but still them. He also heard what the young man said, three words, soft and distant though they were: his own name.

The Cabinet of Wonders

This is the second in a series of unusual, exciting and thoughtful stories:

1.   Philip
2.   Lisi
3.   Louey

See the Hawkwood Books website for more details.

Notes

This might be a story but Sir Isaac Newton was real. Of course, you knew that. His name drifts down the years. He was brilliant, creative, brave and tireless, but he was also, once, a child. I hope I've captured a little of that lost boy. Some of the scenes are based around events that really did happen and places that really existed, but it is still fiction. As far as I know, we can't step through mysterious archways to the past. If you want to get to know the real man, there are many books about his life and many more web pages. Take a look. You might meet him as clearly as Lisi and Laszlo. I doubt he'll need your help but he might help you. You never know.